MARY INGALLS
ON HER OWN

LITTLE HOUSE · BIG ADVENTURE

MARY INGALLS
ON HER OWN

by ELIZABETH KIMMEL WILLARD

HarperCollins*Publishers*

Mary Ingalls on Her Own
Copyright © 2008 by HarperCollins Publishers, Inc.
All rights reserved. Printed in the United States of America. No part of
this book may be used or reproduced in any manner whatsoever without
written permission except in the case of brief quotations embodied in crit-
ical articles and reviews. For information address HarperCollins
Children's Books, a division of HarperCollins Publishers, 1350 Avenue of
the Americas, New York, NY 10019.
www.littlehousebooks.com

Library of Congress Cataloging-in-Publication Data
Kimmel, Elizabeth Cody.
    Mary Ingalls on her own / by Elizabeth Kimmel Willard. — 1st ed.
        p.   cm.
    Summary: In 1881, sixteen-year-old Mary Ingalls becomes a student at
the Iowa College for the Blind, where she studies academic subjects and
learns skills that will allow her to be independent and to earn a living.
    ISBN 978-0-06-000905-2 (trade bdg.)
    ISBN 978-0-06-000906-9 (lib. bdg.)
    [1. Blind—Fiction. 2. People with disabilities—Fiction. 3. Schools—
Fiction. 4. Interpersonal relations—Fiction.] I. Title.
PZ7.K56475Mar 2008   2007010908
[Fic]—dc22   CIP
                                                              AC

Typography by Christopher Stengel
1 2 3 4 5 6 7 8 9 10

First Edition

For Emma Cody Kimmel, with love

CONTENTS

MARY INGALLS
ON HER OWN

College Girl

Mary Ingalls stepped carefully from the train onto the bustling platform in Vinton, Iowa. She stood straight and quiet, her hands clasping the handle of her small suitcase. Her pale blue eyes shone with a mix of anxiety and excitement. Mary took a deep breath as the cool November breeze fanned her flushed cheeks and carried the hot smell of engine steam past her nose.

Over the noise of the hissing steam, Mary heard the sound of Pa's voice calling to her. Her Ma gently took her by the elbow, and not for the first time that day, Mary felt relieved that both her parents had made this journey with her. Nothing here felt the same as it had back in her hometown of De Smet. Dakota Territory itself seemed to be a completely different world.

"Iowa College for the Blind!" called a deep voice. "This way for students of Iowa College for the Blind!"

With a start, Mary realized that she was one of the students the man was calling for. She felt pink with embarrassment. Now everyone at the station would know she was a blind girl. She wondered if anyone had stopped to stare at her.

"They've sent a buggy for us," Ma said, leading Mary along. As they walked, Mary could hear the sound of a horse nickering and shifting impatiently from hoof to hoof. Pa called out a pleasant greeting to the driver.

"Do you see any other students, Ma, or am I the only one?" Mary whispered.

There was a pause.

"I don't see anyone who looks . . . who seems to be coming along with us, Mary. We are the only ones who have come to the buggy."

"I'll take that bag, young lady," said the same deep voice that Mary had heard before. The little suitcase was lifted out of her hands. Mary felt self-conscious, smoothing her dress and straightening her bonnet. She realized she ought to thank the man, but she didn't know if he had already walked to the back of the buggy to load the luggage, or if he was still standing nearby. Before she could decide what to do, Ma thanked the man for his help.

Mary hated not knowing what to do. Back home, she knew the sound and smell of every street in De Smet and could make her way around town almost as well as anyone. But everything in Iowa was different. For the first time since the scarlet fever had taken her eyesight almost two years earlier, Mary Ingalls was without her sisters in an unfamiliar place.

She felt for Ma's hand where it still held her elbow, and she squeezed it tightly.

The road from the train station to the school was well traveled, and the buggy's springs helped keep the ride from getting too bumpy.

Still, Mary's stomach felt tight and sour, and though the cool air smelled pleasantly of grass and earth, her hands were slick and her face hot. Mary thought about the train journey, and about the fried blackbirds they had eaten for lunch. They were the very same birds that had recently devoured Pa's corn crop. The Ingalls family had gotten their revenge, because Ma had cooked those birds and packed them in a shoebox to bring on the train. They had made a good meal, but now they were making Mary feel ill. She reminded herself how lucky she was that Ma had brought a filling lunch for them—how lucky she was that Ma and Pa had both come along on the train with her. But somehow this only reminded Mary of the three sisters she had left behind.

If Laura were here, Mary thought, she would be my eyes for me, just as she always is. She would be talking nonstop, describing the land and all the houses and farms she could see. Mary imagined the sound of Laura's voice counting each fence post as they passed it, so that Mary would know how fast the buggy was going.

When the driver called back to them that they were nearing the school, Mary's heart jumped with nervousness. For some reason, it hadn't seemed quite real until now. There were so many things to think about—so many things that might go wrong. Though students could begin at the college at any time during the year, most of the students had begun classes two months ago, in September. Mary's family had had to wait to be sure they had all of the first year's tuition money. Would the other girls have already made friends? Would they like Mary at all?

There was also the worrisome fact of Mary's entrance examinations, which were scheduled for the next day. The Ingallses' old friend Reverend Alden had all but ensured Mary's acceptance, sending her school records and a glowing letter of recommendation to the college. The exams were really just a formality, she'd been told, but passing them was a requirement for official acceptance. Mary wished she had been able to take them at home in De Smet. Everything was so strange and different here. The tests might be different from those she was used to. How could she expect her brain to work properly? She might do badly on the exams. If she did, would she be sent home in disgrace?

On the seat beside her, Mary could feel Ma sitting up straighter to get a better look at the school. Mary stopped herself from thinking about doing badly on the exams. She took in the smell of the cool country air, and she smiled. She wanted Ma and Pa to know that she was happy to be arriving at college.

"Can you see the school, Ma?" Mary asked.

"Oh yes I can, Mary!" Ma cried. "It's beautiful. Isn't it, Charles?"

"It certainly is," Pa said. "It looks like a castle, Mary. The building is all brick, three stories high, and there is a wing built on either side. No blizzard wind will be getting through those walls!"

Mary thought of the terrible blizzards they had endured last year in Dakota Territory. She had spent the winter with her parents and her sisters, Laura, Carrie, and Grace, huddled together in the house. Mary had helped grind wheat for Ma to bake into bread, while Laura and Pa had made hay twists to burn in the fire when the wood ran out. How she would miss her sisters and her home!

"You make the school sound like a drawing from a fairy-tale book, Pa," Mary said, trying to sound cheerful.

"Each wing has two verandas, and there is a tower on top of the roof, Mary," Ma told her. "There are lovely trees out front, and gravel paths across each lawn. Perhaps you can take walks, just as you do at home with Laura."

Mary smiled.

"I hope so, Ma," she replied.

"Excuse me, miss," came the driver's voice. "We'll be pulling around the back of the main building. I'll see to your things, and you and your folks can go on inside to meet the principal."

Mary wanted to ask the driver if he knew what sort of man the principal was. Was he very strict or easygoing? Young or elderly? Did he have children of his own? But that would be rude. Mary would meet him herself soon enough.

Mary felt the buggy slowly come to a halt. Ma squeezed her arm and asked, "Are you ready to be a college girl now, Mary?"

"Of course I am, Ma," Mary replied. She said it because she knew that was what Ma wanted to hear, but truthfully, Mary felt overwhelmed with anxiety at the thought of being left alone in this big new place. She had told Laura during their last walk together that she was afraid she would be lonely at school, but Mary did not confide the same feelings to Ma. Ma would only worry, and Mary was worried enough for them both.

"That's my good girl," Ma said. Mary could hear the smile in Ma's voice, and she was glad she had kept her fears to herself.

The sitting room in the main building was warm and cozy, and Mary smelled the comforting scent of burning wood.

"It's nice to have the fire," Mary remarked. "It makes the room feel like home to have a woodstove."

Pa chuckled. "I hadn't even noticed the

stove. You pick up these things so quickly now, Mary. It's a wonder you don't know the color of the wallpaper."

"I don't know the color, but since this is a sitting room for guests, I'd guess it has little flowers," Mary said quickly.

Pa shouted with laughter. "Well I'll be blamed! It does have flowers at that!"

"Charles," Ma said quietly. "We mustn't raise our voices."

Pa kept chuckling, but more softly now. Mary heard footsteps coming down the hall— the solid, heavy footsteps of a man. She removed her gloves and raised one hand to check that her hair was still neatly pulled back. Ma always said how important first impressions were, and Mary wanted to make a good one. At home, Laura often remarked that Mary never had a hair out of place, and Mary was proud that losing her eyesight had not changed this. If only she could have worn her best cashmere dress. Ma had made it especially for college, and Mary knew that she looked lovely in it. But it was not yet cold enough for a winter dress, so she had made do with her old calico.

"The calico suits you nicely," Ma whispered, and Mary smiled. As usual, Ma seemed to know when Mary was worried about how she looked. Mary sat up straighter as she heard the footsteps come right into the room.

"Hello, hello," came a man's pleasant voice. "You must be the Ingalls family."

Mary stood up carefully, holding her gloves in one hand.

"I am Mr. Carothers, the principal of the college."

Mary waited while Ma and Pa introduced themselves, and then it was her turn. Inwardly, she was so nervous, she felt as if her whole body must be shaking.

"I am Mary Ingalls. I'm very pleased to meet you, Mr. Carothers, and to be here at the college."

"Thank you, Mary," came his reply. "Please sit down, all of you."

Mary flicked her hand toward the back of the chair to check its position. She kept one hand on the chair as she sat down. When Mr.

Carothers began to speak again, Mary could tell that he had remained standing from the direction of the sound of his voice.

"First of all, Mary, I'd like to welcome you to the college. This is a very special place, one where people who put their minds to it can accomplish things they might not have thought possible before enrolling. You will have two roommates. One of them is in class at the moment, and the other is in the infirmary with a rather bad cold, but you will meet them both in due course. They are lovely girls, and I'm sure you'll get on very well."

Mary nodded in agreement, hoping that Mr. Carothers was right.

"You will be taking academic classes, of course, but you will also be learning skills that will enable you to one day earn an income of your own. Our students learn to make brooms and fly nets, to knit and do beadwork, and several are even learning to become piano tuners. When you leave this college, you will not be educated solely in academics—you will have learned what you need to be independent, a valuable trait indeed."

Mary nodded again. Her family had told her she would always be cared for, and she loved them for it. But Mary longed to learn a skill that could provide her with work and money for her family. She was blind, yes, but one day she might be less of a burden to her family.

"That being said," Mr. Carothers continued, "I want to give you the same advice I give all our new students. This is a learning institution, and that is what you are here to do—to learn. You are a beginner, and you must not be too proud to ask for help. Sometimes new students can be headstrong and determined to show that they can accomplish things right away without any assistance. More often than not, this leads to trouble, and the occasional accident. Ask questions, Mary, and seek assistance when you need it. Let yourself be guided. I cannot stress that enough."

There was a pause, and Mary felt she ought to reply. Despite Mr. Carothers' advice, Mary had already determined that she would not make mistakes, and that she would learn faster than anyone else and require less help than most new students. But she could hardly say so. Mary nodded politely and said, "Yes, Mr. Carothers. I understand."

"Very good, then," he replied. "I believe that's all for now. Mary, your college advisor, Miss Mattice, will visit you in your room tomorrow to answer any questions you have. Miss Mattice is one of our most beloved teachers, and she will also help you with your exams tomorrow. We usually like our advisors to escort new students to their rooms after they arrive, but Miss Mattice is in an Advisory Council meeting and is unable to come now. Perhaps your parents would like to escort you instead."

"That would be lovely," said Ma. Mary heard the rustle of Ma's skirts as she stood.

"Mr. and Mrs. Ingalls, if you walk out of this room and into the main hallway, you will see a wide wooden staircase under the stained-glass window. Take the left branch of that staircase up two flights, and go left down the hallway. Please show Mary that there is a guide rail on each side of the hall. You should use the guide rail, Mary, until you get used to walking here. Most students know exactly how many steps it is to their room without even counting consciously after only a few weeks. Mary's door will be the fourth door on the right. Don't count the small gray door, as that is only a supply closet."

"Thank you, sir," Pa said. Mary suddenly smelled a little of his pipe tobacco scent, and knew he had stepped closer to her.

"Yes, thank you for everything, Mr. Carothers," Ma said.

"Not at all," he replied. "Welcome, Mary." Mary listened as his footsteps faded.

"Well, Mary, what do you think?" Pa asked. His voice was hearty, as if he were trying extra hard to be cheerful. "Are you ready to go to your new room?"

"I'm ready, Pa," Mary replied. She was a little anxious to know what her room would be like, and to meet the girls she would be living so closely with. Trying to appear calm and unafraid was exhausting. But she must do it.

Her family had made a great many sacrifices to raise the money to pay for this school. Laura had worked long hours sewing, giving every cent she earned to Ma for the college fund. Pa had sold their heifer calf, and each Ingalls had gone without something so that another penny could be put away for Mary. It would only be when Ma and Pa left Mary in her room today that she could finally stop worrying that her hands were trembling, or that her brow was wrinkled in an anxious frown.

Mary felt a familiar touch on her elbow as Ma gently led her out of the college's sitting room. Pa walked ahead of them, whistling an Irish tune softly.

The main hall was solemn and still, though in the distance were the faint sounds of many voices talking. Mary thought those must be from the classes in session. She felt the sun on her face, and smelled the scent of fresh air creeping through a drafty window. Mary paused and reached out a hand toward the warmth of the sunshine, but she was not close enough to the window to touch it.

"Here is the stairway," Pa said. Ma tightened her grip just slightly on Mary's elbow, indicating that they'd come to the first step. Mary reached out with her left hand and found the banister, smooth and well-worn. At the top of the first flight of stairs was a small landing, and Mary kept her hand on the banister as they walked around and began climbing the second flight of stairs.

"Here is your hall, Mary," Ma said. "If you take just four steps to your right, you can find the guide rail Mr. Carothers mentioned. It looks as if there must be twenty or so rooms on this wing. At the very end of the hall I see a window. The rail is on both sides of the corridor, at about the height of your waist."

Ma let Mary's elbow go, to let her find her own way from the landing to the hallway, as she would need to do later. Mary walked carefully, both hands gingerly extended. It used to feel so embarrassing to walk around with her hands out in front of her body. It reminded her of the games of blindman's buff they played at recess in school, when Mary was a girl. But she'd had to overcome that. It would be more embarrass-ing, after all, to walk into a wall.

After several steps, she felt the smooth wall of the hallway. The railing was where Ma had described. Mary was almost to her room. It was just four doors away. Suddenly Mary's hands began to shake badly, and she gripped the rail-ing tightly to hide the tremble. Her heart began pounding in her chest, and she felt a lump rise in her throat.

I'm going to cry, Mary thought. But I mustn't. Not while Ma and Pa are here.

"I can find my room now," Mary said, her voice coming out too fast and high.

"Why, don't be silly, Mary," Pa said. "It's not much more than twenty feet away. We can walk with you."

"I know, Pa," Mary said quickly. "But I'd like to do this myself. You'll be going home in just a few days, and I'd like to start off on the right foot. Doing something independently. You said yourself it's only twenty feet or so."

Mary could tell Pa was hesitating.

"It's what she wants to do, Charles," Ma

said, her voice soft but firm.

"All right, then," Pa said. "Of course, Mary. Ma and I can go over to our hotel. We'll be back tomorrow, to see you after your exams."

"We can meet in the sitting room downstairs, where we met the principal," Ma added.

Ma hugged Mary, and Mary swallowed hard. She felt the touch of Pa's big, strong hand on her shoulder.

"Good-bye, Ma. Good-bye, Pa. I'll see you tomorrow morning," Mary said. She thought it was amazing that she could even pretend to sound cheerful. She turned, her hand back on the guide rail, and moved carefully down the hallway. She felt Ma's and Pa's eyes on her for a moment, then heard them walk back to the landing and begin going down the stairs. Mary wanted to sob with both relief and sadness.

Not yet, she told herself. I must get to the room. I must concentrate.

Mary took several steps, then felt a break in the guide rail. There was a door. She traced her fingers lightly over the door's surface, feeling mottled paint, and in three steps the guide rail began again.

This won't be hard, Mary thought. My door is the fourth on the right. Only three away from here.

Mary kept walking, feeling a second, smoother door, then a third. The hallway was strangely quiet. The students must all be in their classes downstairs. That was good, Mary decided. She could go into her room before anyone returned, and find her way around it. By the time she met her roommates, she would know what was where.

When Mary came to the fourth door, she stopped, then ran her hand over the wood until she found the doorknob. Mary paused, taking a deep breath.

She opened the door and walked inside.

Immediately, a voice cried out loudly and angrily.

"Here! What do you think you're doing barging into my room?"

MATTIE

The voice startled Mary, as she was expecting the room to be empty. She let out a small shriek of surprise and stumbled, colliding with a heavy piece of furniture. Mary lost her balance and flung her arms out to catch herself. Her right arm hit something, which fell onto the floor with an explosion of little sounds, like hail on a wooden roof.

Now the voice screamed in anger.

"My beads! What have you done? I've taken hours to sort them, and you've knocked them all onto the floor—you stupid, stupid girl!"

Mary opened her mouth, but nothing came out.

"What are you doing in my room?" the voice demanded.

Mary straightened her skirt nervously, and swallowed to ease the lump in her throat.

"I'm . . . I'm a new student. Mary Ingalls," she said. Her voice was tight and high. "I thought this was my room. Isn't it? I counted the doors."

"Well you counted wrong, Mary Ingalls," came the response. She said Mary's name in a cold, mocking way. "This is *my* room, and I don't share with anyone. I haven't got to. You must be with Blanche and Hannah next door. You didn't go far enough. How did you get accepted into college when you can't even count?"

Mary felt shocked and speechless. The last thing she had expected was an outburst like this. But Ma would tell her she must be the one to rise above. And it seemed she *had* made a mistake.

"I'm sorry," Mary said. Her voice sounded a

bit more normal now. "And I'm sorry for knocking over your beads. I can help you pick them up."

"And make things even worse? No thank you."

Mary bit her lip. When one apologized to a person, they ought to be forgiving. Mary didn't like this spiteful girl at all. Rise above, she thought, picturing Ma's face.

"Why are you still standing there? Go away, Mary Ingalls."

That suggestion suited Mary quite well. She wanted nothing more than to get out of this room and away from this horrible girl. And since everything she said only seemed to make the girl angrier, Mary turned in silence to go. She felt the open door and walked out, pulling it closed behind her.

Mary took a moment to compose herself in the hallway. Then, carefully running her fingers along the wall, she walked on until she found the next door. This time, Mary knocked. When no one answered, she knocked louder. Only when she was sure no one was inside did she open the door.

Mary stood in the doorway a moment, then stepped inside.

Her heart was still beating quickly from the unpleasant encounter next door. She couldn't understand how she had ended up in the wrong room. She had counted four doors, so how could there have been a mistake?

Then Mary's heart sank. Mr. Carothers had told Ma and Pa about a small supply-closet door. Now that she thought about it, the first door Mary touched *had* felt different from the others. But she had counted it as the first room, and that was how she had ended up in the wrong place. How foolish I am, Mary thought. The very first thing I do alone at school ends up being completely wrong.

As she stood there running her mistake over and over again in her mind, she became aware of warm sunshine on her face. Mary loved sunny rooms, because they felt so cheerful. She wondered—was her room big? How many windows? As Mary closed the door, her fingers touched something on the back of it. Mounted on the back of the door was a framed paper covered with little raised bumps in lines. She thought at first it must be some kind of decoration, but then Mary remembered Reverend Alden describing a special raised print invented for the blind. Maybe by Christmas she would be able to read raised print such as this.

Mary walked carefully across the room, her hands reaching high then low to search for furniture, a trunk, anything that might trip her up. She noticed a rug under her feet, which she bent down to touch. It was a rag rug, like the one Mary had made during the long winter of blizzards in Dakota Territory. She had worked for hours cutting bits of wool and braiding them together to make that rug, listening to the banshee screams of the wind outside. Mary had worked through the darkest hours of the storm, even when Laura had to stop sewing her lace because there was not enough light to see. Mary had been able to do something her sighted sister could not.

Mary touched the neat, tiny stitches where

this rug had been sewn together, and remembered how Laura had sewn the braids together in Mary's rug. And when she was finished, she had placed it over Mary's legs to keep her warm. Laura always looked out for her. If only Laura were here, Mary thought, I wouldn't be so afraid.

But Laura was not here, nor would she be coming. There was no point in dwelling on it. Mary continued to explore. Her foot connected with a solid object, and she bent down to feel it. It had a tin-covered lid with bumps pressed into patterns of leaves and flowers. Between the tin places were strips of smooth, well oiled wood. Her trunk! And next to it was the small suitcase she had carried on the train. With everything so new and strange, it was a relief to find a bit of home in the room. And it left no question that she was now in the right place.

The trunk was set at the foot of a bed. Mary walked the length of it, tracing her fingers over a quilt. On her left was a second bed. When the admission letter from the college had come to Ma and Pa, it had said that most rooms housed three or four students, with two to a bed where necessary.

Mary had always loved sharing a bed with Laura. The extra warmth and bedtime whispering were fun. But sharing a bed with a roommate would be very strange. Mary hated the idea that she would have to worry about her behavior even while she slept. Laura often teased her for kicking, or sometimes even snoring in the night. She didn't mind Laura's teasing, but it would be horribly embarrassing to kick or snore next to a stranger! For that matter, what if it was her *bedmate* who was a kicker or a snorer? She couldn't worry about that now. Mary sighed and continued exploring.

Working her way around the room, Mary found a chest of drawers near the door. Opening the top drawer, Mary put her hand inside and touched something lacy, perhaps a petticoat. She immediately pulled her hand away and closed the drawer. It felt like snooping, even though Mary was only looking for a place to put her things.

The bottom drawer was empty. Good, Mary thought. Now she had something to do. She could unpack her things and put everything away. Pa had put the key to Mary's trunk on a string, which she was wearing around her neck. She put the key in the padlock and opened the trunk, which she had packed herself. But unpacking took much less time than Mary had hoped, and within minutes she was finished.

Ma always said that putting one's things away in a new place made it seem like home. Her family had lived in many places. Wisconsin, Missouri, Kansas, Minnesota. The Ingallses had even lived here in Iowa for a time, a few years before finally settling down for good in Dakota Territory. Each time they moved to a new place, whether it was a sod dugout or a log cabin, Ma would place her china shepherdess on the mantel when everything else had been unpacked. And that was how the Ingalls family knew they were home again.

But Mary didn't have a personal token like the china shepherdess, and with nothing more to do, she sat on the edge of the bed, and her thoughts returned to the nasty girl in the next room. Though she still felt she had done the right thing in keeping her temper and being polite, Mary was astonished by the girl's meanness. One just didn't shout at people that way. One certainly didn't call a person stupid. What if there were other people at the college like that—even Mary's roommates?

No, Mary told herself. Everything was going to be fine. Her roommates would be like her friends at home—sweet and even tempered. She was finally at college, and she should be happy about it. Laura and Ma had spent hours helping her study for the entrance examination she would take tomorrow. Mary had always been an excellent student, and her fingers were as nimble as her mind. She was a very good seamstress, so she would probably be good at the broom- and net-making classes Mr. Carothers had mentioned. Mary took in a good, deep breath. She was going to do well and make Ma and Pa proud. Her roommates would like her, and she would like them. And that girl next door would find out sooner or later that no matter what she thought, Mary Ingalls was not a stupid girl.

It must be nearly five o'clock by now, Mary thought. It should be time for supper soon. Where was everyone? It was so frustrating not to be able to *do* anything.

She would just have to sit there until somebody finally came for her.

A Warm Welcome

The silence in the huge building began to sound ominous as she waited. Where were all the people? Ma had described a long hallway, door after door leading to students' rooms, and classrooms somewhere on the lower floors. She knew there were almost one hundred students enrolled at the college, and many teachers and assistants, but at that moment Mary felt as if she were the only living soul in this great brick castle she must now call home. In De Smet, Mary had cherished the rare quiet moments when Grace was sleeping and Laura and Carrie were taking a walk or doing outside chores. But now the silence seemed to have little fingers that poked and prodded and gave Mary goose bumps. As she was beginning to think she must make some noise herself or she would go mad, the distant sounds of bells reached her ears. Within moments, Mary heard many voices laughing and calling to one another.

Mary had been anxious for her roommates to return, but now that the door might open at any moment, she felt a nervous flutter in her stomach. Things had started out so badly with the girl next door. What if the same thing happened with Blanche or Hannah?

The sounds of merry chattering and footsteps were much closer now. Mary sat on the edge of the bed and smoothed her skirts. Her heart raced. Stop being nervous, Mary told herself. She hated this, everything being so new, so unfamiliar. Laura would probably consider it a big adventure, but Mary would not be happy or at ease until she knew her roommates, learned her way around the school, and mastered her classes. Mary Ingalls did not like surprises. And she did not like being away from home.

The door opened suddenly, and Mary jumped.

"Hello?" Mary asked.

"You're here! Mr. Carothers told us you'd be coming this afternoon. Has Miss Mattice come to greet you yet? You are Mary Ingalls, aren't you?" The girlish voice sounded kind.

Mary stood up and smiled.

"Yes, I'm Mary. Are you Blanche or Hannah?"

The girl walked over to the bed, and Mary felt two warm hands clasp her own.

"I'm Blanche. Hannah has the most terrible cold—she's been in the infirmary for two days. Have you been waiting here long? Did your folks come with you? What soft hands you have!"

Blanche's friendly questions tumbled out so quickly, and her voice was so merry and warm, Mary almost laughed aloud with relief.

"I haven't been waiting too long. My folks have gone over to their hotel."

"And have you met Miss Mattice yet? We all

just adore her—it's like having another ma."

"I'm to meet her tomorrow," Mary replied. "My folks brought me upstairs."

Mary hesitated a moment, then, almost before she realized it, told Blanche the whole story.

"I asked Ma and Pa to leave me at the entrance to the hallway, because I had this silly idea that it was important I make my way to the room by myself the first time," Mary began.

Before she could continue, Blanche laughed and squeezed Mary's hands.

"I've never heard of anyone doing that on her first day! I don't think you're silly, I think you're brave! And aren't you lucky you didn't go into Mattie's room next door. She'd have bitten your head off."

Mary laughed.

"Oh, but Blanche, I did! That's exactly what happened! I counted the doors wrong, and opened hers because I thought it was my room. I knocked her beads onto the floor! She was terribly angry and rude."

Mary felt a little guilty about saying these

bad things about Mattie. She had been raised not to gossip about others. But Blanche just laughed sympathetically.

"You poor thing!" Blanche exclaimed. "What a way to be welcomed. I have to tell you that Mattie is always furious with everyone. The very oldest girls are allowed to choose their roommates, but Mattie has scared off so many students, they don't even try to put other girls with her anymore. Apparently she's been given several warnings by the college already. Miss Mattice says she's going through a difficult time and to be patient, but I think she's just mean through and through. To everyone. Promise me you won't mind her."

"I promise," Mary said.

"Come on," Blanche said, linking her arm through Mary's. "I'll take you down to supper. You must be famished after traveling."

"Thank you," Mary said. She was actually far too nervous to be hungry, but she was happy to go anywhere out of this room. She let Blanche lead her to the door. It was such a relief to let somebody else be in charge. And

Blanche seemed sweet and lovely. Mary thought she couldn't have asked for a nicer roommate.

They walked into the hallway and back toward the staircase. As they walked down the stairs, Mary heard the voices of other girls all around her. She sensed them walking past and wondered if they knew she was there.

"Is your ma a good cook?" Blanche asked.

"Oh, yes!" replied Mary, thoughts of Ma's white biscuits and crisp-crusted apple pie filling her head.

"Well, you'll certainly miss that," Blanche said with a laugh. "The food here is pretty plain, but it isn't so bad when you get used to it. It's just not very . . . interesting."

At the foot of the staircase, they turned and walked into a hallway. Mary could smell food, and the sounds of voices, boys' as well as girls' now, grew much louder. Mary was gladder than ever to have Blanche's arm to hold on to. She squeezed a little tighter than she meant to as they walked through a doorway into the dining hall. Even so, she brushed against the doorjamb with her arm.

"You'll be here, at my table," said Blanche. "Hannah will sit here too, when she's well enough to leave the infirmary. The tables are long rectangles, and we sit eight to a side. The boys sit on the other side of the dining room at their own tables. Did they tell you that you are meant to bring your own napkins?"

"Yes," Mary replied, pulling one of the linen napkins Ma had given her out of her pocket.

"Good," said Blanche. "Sometimes the new girls forget. Sit next to me, Mary. Miss Stanton is in charge of meals. She'll be poking about somewhere, so beware. And Mr. McCune, the head administrator, he's the man with the raspy voice, says the blessing before we eat. Our food is always served the same way—meat at the bottom center of the plate, vegetable on the right, and biscuit on the left. Use the biscuit to help guide the food onto your fork. You must be very careful not to spill on the tablecloth. Miss Stanton would forgive you on your first day, but if you did it again, you'd have to eat with your plate on an oilcloth for a week to prove you'd learned to be tidy!"

I don't need to worry, Mary told herself. I never lose track of so much as a crumb at home.

The voices around the room hushed as a man began speaking. That must be Mr. McCune. Mary bowed her head as he gave the blessing. When he finished, the room broke out in quiet but cheerful talk.

A plate of food was passed to Mary. She placed it in front of her, and explored it gingerly with her fork.

"Chicken," Blanche said helpfully. Mary could smell it then, and she lightly ran her fork around the chicken until she knew the size and cut of the meat. She probed to the right and recognized the vegetable as green beans. And on the left was a biscuit, just as Blanche had said it would be.

"Girls, this is my new roommate, Mary Ingalls," Blanche said. Mary heard a chorus of hellos, and several questions.

"I'm Charlotte, Mary. Across from you and one seat to your right. Have you only just arrived?"

Mary had a bite of biscuit in her mouth, which she chewed as quickly as she could, but when she swallowed, it made a painful lump traveling down her throat.

"Yes, Charlotte, I arrived this afternoon. I've come from De Smet, in Dakota Territory."

As soon as Mary paused, the voices started up again, like a flock of birds.

"Did you take the train?" asked one.

"Are your folks here? Do you have a big family?" asked another.

"Girls, girls, for mercy's sake!" cried Blanche. "You'll have Mary's head spinning and she'll end up in the infirmary with Hannah!"

Mary appreciated Blanche's good-natured tone, and the way she kept trying to make things easier for Mary. She tried to remember all the questions she'd just been asked.

"I did take the train, with my Ma and Pa," Mary said. "They are staying overnight here in Vinton and will be leaving after my entrance examinations are graded. I have three sisters at home, and I'm going to miss them very much. But I'm glad to be here at college," Mary added.

She took a breath, and there was a lull. Then came a hard-edged voice that she recognized.

"What's wrong with your eyes?"

Mary froze, her fork poised over the chicken.

"What's wrong with them? They don't look sickly. Can you see at all? Because you don't act like it."

"Mattie, how rude," Blanche cried. "Don't mind her, Mary. She asks all the new girls that, no matter how often we remind her to be more polite."

No one had ever asked Mary directly about her eyesight before. It had always been obvious, or maybe Ma and Pa had discreetly explained to people when Mary wasn't listening. But no one had ever been so ill-bred as to ask Mary bluntly what was wrong with her. And what did Mattie mean about Mary's eyes not looking sickly, or asking if she could see at all? Wasn't Mattie supposed to be blind as well? All the voices at the table had fallen silent. I might as well just answer, Mary thought.

"I took ill with scarlet fever two years ago. I was extremely ill—the doctor thought I might not live. Luckily, I did get better, and the only damage was the complete loss of my sight."

To Mary's astonishment, Mattie laughed out loud.

"'The only damage was the complete loss of my sight,'" Mattie mimicked. "Another precious optimist. I bet you'd always look on the sunny side, Mary, if you weren't blind as a bat."

"Hold your tongue, Mattie," cried Charlotte. Several other voices chimed in, telling Mattie to be quiet.

"I won't, and you can't make me," Mattie said defiantly. "But I won't waste any more of my breath, either. Not with a stupid girl who actually sounds thankful to be blind. If I were blind, you can be certain I wouldn't be chirping so happily about it."

"What do you mean, *if* you were blind?" Mary asked, her curiosity overcoming her shyness. Surely they were all blind, weren't they? Mattie did not reply. Mary opened her mouth to repeat the question louder, then stopped herself. Oh, what was happening? Mary had meant to eat very quietly and only speak if she was spoken to. Now she was having words with Mattie in front of the entire table!

"Mattie isn't entirely blind right now," Charlotte explained. "She has a disease of the cornea. When it's light, she can still see things that are close. So she considers herself superior to those of us who can't see at all."

"What Charlotte means is that I don't think I belong here. And I don't! I will never go blind and stumble around like the rest of you," Mattie said angrily. Then came the sound of a chair being pushed back from the table.

"Better not let Miss Stanton catch you leaving your supper early," Blanche called. But Mattie had gone. "Oh, never mind. We're better off without her."

"Dreadful girl," Charlotte said, and several girls murmured in agreement.

"But Mattie can really see a little?" Mary asked, her curiosity getting the better of her.

"Yes, she can," Blanche said. "For the time being. So can I, as you mention it. I can still make out some shapes, and even colors if they are in a very bright light. I don't know a lot about Mattie's disease, but I do know it is expected to get worse until she is fully blind. But Mattie doesn't want to believe she's in the same boat as the rest of us."

"Why did she say my eyes didn't look sickly?" Mary asked.

"Mattie's condition has caused her eyes to cloud over," Blanche explained. "So they look milky and odd. Many of us here have eyes that look damaged—a person could tell some of us were blind just by looking. But scarlet fever doesn't damage the outside of the eye. I'm sure you look much as you always did, Mary. And judging from how angry Mattie gets around you, I can guess you have very pretty eyes indeed."

Mary had always been told since she was a little girl that she had clear, beautiful eyes of a startling pale blue, and Blanche was right, Laura told Mary that she looked just the same as she had before going blind. Ma had cut off all of Mary's long blond hair when she was sick to help relieve the fever, but by now it had grown almost as long as it used to be. Mary didn't think about being pretty, especially now that she was blind. But she knew that people thought of her that way, which made her *feel* good. And Mattie, with her strange milky eyes, obviously didn't share that self-confidence.

"Mattie is here because her doctors have told her she will go completely blind one day," explained Charlotte. "I suppose her family felt it was better to get her started at the college while some of her sight still remained. Mattie doesn't seem to agree."

"And you said you aren't fully blind either, Blanche?" Mary asked.

"Yes, that's right. A person who can see only a little needs just as much help adjusting as a person who can't see at all. For my part, I'm here both to learn to care for myself being partially blind and to prepare for the time that my sight might fail completely."

"Will that happen?" Mary asked curiously.

"I don't know," Blanche admitted. "Only time will tell. I've made my peace with it. And if and when I do lose the rest of my sight, I shall already know Braille—which you'll learn, Mary. It's a way of reading by touching raised dots. And I'll have learned how to take care of myself and do what needs doing without using my eyes."

"Oh, Blanche, that must be so hard for you. Never knowing what might happen to your sight," Mary said.

"Not really, Mary," Blanche said in her quiet, kind voice. "I'm very happy here. I have Hannah. And now I have you! Don't let Mattie get to you. She's just a terribly angry person, always ready to boil over. Know what you can expect from her, and don't take it personally. Anyway, she usually steers clear of the rest of us. She won't always be as much of a bother as she was just now."

Mary smiled, but she couldn't help but feel a little disappointed to know such an unpleasant girl would be around every day. Of course, Mary reminded herself, one couldn't expect all the girls to be nice. Mary suddenly saw the face of sneering, haughty Nellie Oleson in her mind's eye. The faces she had known in childhood were still as clear in her mind as ever— even vicious Nellie, who had been so cruel to

Laura. Though in the end, Laura had always managed to get the upper hand. Mary almost laughed out loud at the memory of some of Laura's pranks on Nellie.

But Laura was not here, Mary reminded herself again. The best thing to do about Mattie was to stay as far away from her as possible. Mary promised herself to bite her tongue and have patience, and hope that she and Mattie did not rub elbows too often.

Entrance Examinations

"Mary," a voice called softly. "Mary. Do wake up. You don't want to be late."

Mary sat up in bed, clutching the quilt to her chest. She knew she was not at home, but for a moment she could not remember where she was.

"Thank goodness you're sitting up," said Blanche. "You were sleeping like a log."

Blanche was obviously already out of bed. Within minutes of getting under the covers last night, Mary had fallen into a deep, dreamless sleep. All that worrying about sharing a bed with a strange girl, and now that she had done it, Mary couldn't remember any part of it.

"You'll have to hurry and get dressed," Blanche continued. "Miss Mattice will be here soon to get you. Are you nervous, Mary? I know I was."

The entrance examinations! Mary got out of bed quickly and found her way to the chest of drawers to get her clothes. Blanche hovered close by, chattering gaily. Mary was thankful for the distraction. It helped to keep her mind off the examinations.

It was important to Mary that she do well. And she knew that being too confident was dangerous. She had never forgotten the time she had declared there was no need to study for a history test because she always got a perfect score. The test had contained several questions Mary could not answer, and she had hardly been able to bear the look of surprise and disappointment on her parents' faces when she brought home a low grade. Ma and Pa had been disappointed not because Mary had done poorly, but because she had made errors that could easily have been avoided had she studied.

She had never made the mistake of taking her knowledge for granted again.

Though Mary had not attended school in the two years since going blind, she had worked every night on Laura's lessons, which helped keep her sharp. The girls had spent hours quizzing each other on math, spelling, and history. She hoped they had covered all of the scholastic ground that would be needed for Mary's entrance exam, because now there was no more time to study. Mary would just have to keep her mind focused when the time came.

"If you like," Blanche was saying, "I can take you downstairs right now for a quick breakfast."

Mary shook her head, then remembered she had to stop doing that. She was not in a house full of sighted folks now. She needed to use her voice.

"No thank you, Blanche. It's thoughtful of you to offer, but I already have butterflies in my stomach. I couldn't eat a thing. I'll just wait here until Miss Mattice comes for me."

"Don't worry about the exam, Mary,"

Blanche said. "That's easier said than done, I know—*I* worried like anything about it! Some of the questions are tough, but if you are up-to-date on your studies, you can manage them. Do you know what I did? I pretended I wasn't taking a test, but that I was at a sociable. And another girl was asking me questions. I simply answered them as if we were having a friendly conversation!"

Mary smiled. "That's a good idea, Blanche," she said.

"And it worked, too," Blanche said eagerly. "Though Miss Mattice did find it a bit strange. She didn't say so at the time, but she told me later she couldn't understand why I kept smiling the way I did. I was too embarrassed to tell her what I'd been pretending, so I explained it by saying I always smiled when I was nervous."

Mary laughed as Blanche gave a detailed imitation of herself giggling at a question about American history.

A knock came sharply on the door, startling both girls.

"Come in," Mary and Blanche said in unison.

"Good morning, Blanche. And you must be Mary Ingalls. I am Miss Mattice."

Miss Mattice had a deep, rich voice that had a soothing effect on the ear. Mary stood up and extended her hand, which Miss Mattice took with both of her own.

"Welcome, Mary. You are a very lucky young woman to be here with us at the College for the Blind. This is a special place. I know it must feel quite strange to be away from home, but most students come to consider the school their second home, and I shouldn't be surprised if you do too. We are here to teach you about all the opportunities life has to offer, Mary."

Mary immediately liked Miss Mattice. Her voice, and the way she touched Mary's arm lightly as she talked, made Mary feel comfortable.

"Are you ready to walk to the examination room, then?"

"Yes, Miss," Mary replied. She still felt nervous, but Mary looked forward to having the exams completed and the entire experience behind her.

"Come along with me, then," Miss Mattice said. "A nice little stroll to get the blood going does wonders for the brain."

"Good-bye, Blanche," Mary said as she felt Miss Mattice take her arm.

"Good-bye, good luck! Remember the sociable!"

"Remember the what?" asked Miss Mattice, a laugh in her voice as she led Mary out the door and down the hall.

"Something Blanche told me so I won't be nervous," Mary explained.

"Are you nervous, Mary? I don't imagine you need be. I've gone over your school records, and you are an exceptional student. I don't think you will have any difficulty today."

"Oh, thank you, Miss," Mary said. It was one thing for Blanche to tell Mary not to worry. But Miss Mattice was a teacher here, and if she said not to worry, Mary felt she could better believe it.

They had descended the staircase as they talked, and turned onto a corridor somewhere off the main hall. From the echoes of their footsteps, Mary guessed the corridor was very long. Every once and again, Mary heard a door open or close.

"The exams are given in one of our classrooms," Miss Mattice said. "It isn't far."

"Will you be in the room with me when I take the test?" Mary asked hopefully.

"I have to be," Miss Mattice said with a laugh. "I'm the one who administers the test, Mary. I will ask the questions and write down your answers."

Mary had hoped that since Miss Mattice had given Blanche the exam, she would give it to Mary as well. With this news, the last bit of nervousness left her stomach, and she breathed a deep sigh of relief. Everything was going to be fine.

They slowed down, and Mary heard Miss Mattice open a door. She led Mary into the examination room and brought her to a chair and table. Running her hand over the table and the back of the chair, Mary made a picture of the room in her mind. There was a row of windows on one wall, and wooden desks arranged in straight lines. Mary sat down. She heard Miss Mattice take the seat across the table.

"Now then, Mary," she began. "As I've said, this will be an oral examination. When you have learned to read Braille and to write on a special slate, you will be able to take your class exams by hand, as you used to."

"Yes, Miss," Mary said, holding her hands tightly together in her lap. She wished she could think of something more interesting to say than "Yes, Miss," but friendly conversation would have to come later. Now was the time for concentration.

"I will ask you to do some arithmetic problems in your head, and to answer a series of questions about geography. You will also be diagramming sentences that I dictate to you. We will discuss literature and political economy. But we will begin with history. Describe the Continental Congress."

Mary knew the answer to this very well, but when she opened her mouth to speak, her mind went blank.

"Take your time, Mary," Miss Mattice said.

"I'm not watching the clock. Try to think about when you first learned about the Continental Congress, and imagine the sound of that teacher's voice, and what the classroom looked like."

Mary thought. But it was not the sound of a teacher's voice that she remembered. Instead, it was Laura's voice that came into her head. How many times had Laura quizzed Mary on her American history? How many evenings had they sat by the fire reciting these facts? Suddenly, the picture was very vivid in Mary's mind—sitting with Laura going over lessons. The fire was crackling in the fireplace, and Ma was making supper. As the image came alive in her mind, Mary remembered.

"The Continental Congress was first convened in 1744, in response to the Intolerable Acts of Parliament."

And the rest came just as easily. Mary answered each question as it came, confidently and thoroughly. And all the while, the sound of the fire and of Pa whistling, the smell of baking bread, and Laura's cheerful presence remained in the forefront of her mind.

Ma and Pa were waiting for Mary in the sitting room where Mr. Carothers had greeted them yesterday. Mary wanted to fling herself into Ma's arms, but of course she did not. She thanked the student who had led her to the study, although she wished it had been Miss Mattice so Ma and Pa could meet her. When the student's footsteps trailed away, Mary turned eagerly to her parents.

"Well, Mary," said Pa cheerfully, "how do you like the college so far?"

Mary wanted to tell them everything at once: how she had gone into the wrong room and made Mattie angry, how sweet Blanche was, and how a student who spilled food must eat off an oilcloth. But since Mary didn't want to tell her parents anything that might cause them to worry, she decided to leave Mattie and the dining hall rules out of it.

"Everything is wonderful, Pa. I've met one

of my roommates, Blanche, and she's really kind and helpful. I know you'll like her. And I took my entrance examinations this morning. Miss Mattice, who will be my advisor, gave the test, and she made me feel quite calm and relaxed. The whole thing was over before I knew it."

"I'm glad to hear it. You'll soon be settled in, then. It's important to us that you feel at home here, Mary," Pa said.

"Your Pa and I want your sisters to have a token of the place in which you're living as well, so we are bringing them a souvenir of Vinton."

"Oh, Ma, they'll be very excited! What did you get them?"

"They are autograph albums," Ma said. "I'm told all the city girls have them now. Laura and Carrie can have their friends write a short verse or message, along with their names, as a keepsake. Laura's has a red cover, and Carrie's is blue, and each page inside is a different color."

They were perfect gifts for Laura and

Carrie. It made Mary smile to imagine their faces when they got the albums.

"Grace is too young for an autograph album," Ma said, "and we wanted to get her something she could enjoy right now."

"We found her a picture book, full of color illustrations of all the countries in the world," Pa continued. "Grace can visit the pyramids in Egypt, or Notre Dame Cathedral in Paris, or the Great Wall of China, and she need never leave De Smet to do it," he finished with a chuckle.

Mary was pleased her sisters would be receiving these unexpected presents, especially since Ma and Pa had bought so many new things for Mary for college. They had gotten her a winter dress, petticoats, and a coat and velvet hat. And of course there was her trunk, which was store-bought. Add to that new shoes and stockings, and train fare, and it seemed to Mary that she was costing her family a small fortune. Pa had even insisted she have some pocket money for the Braille books and special slate she would need to buy. Mary hated that her family had gone without things for such a long time in order to give her so much. Now, finally, her sisters were getting a little something in return.

It was lovely to sit in the cozy room, talking and laughing with Ma and Pa. Once the results of her examinations were final, Mary's acceptance at the college would be official, and Ma and Pa would leave. The Ingallses had moved out of their place in town and onto their land claim a mile from De Smet's center. Laura was fourteen and perfectly capable of taking care of her little sisters, but it was an isolated area with few neighbors to call on. Mary knew it worried her folks to leave the girls alone for the better part of a week. They'd be safe inside their cozy home; still, fire, illness, and accidents were always a worry. Ma and Pa must get home as soon as they could.

Once Ma and Pa were gone, though, Mary would truly be on her own. To complete the full college program took six long years. And there was no money left for her to make visits to De Smet, at least not for now. It would be a year or more before she could be home with her family again. However nice Blanche and Miss Mattice were, this place would never be home.

But she did not need to think about that right now. Ma and Pa were here. Mary would worry about tomorrow when tomorrow came.

An End and a Beginning

Mary pulled the covers up to her chin and rolled slowly onto her side so as not to disturb Blanche, who was already snoring lightly. It had been a long, long day. Once her folks had gone back to their hotel, Mary had joined the other students at their industrial training period. Students were working on broom making, sewing, and other skills that might help them achieve some independence after graduating. For today, Mary was there only to get a feel for the various activities industrial training offered. Presuming she passed her exams, she could then decide what training to take first.

Mary was fairly certain, now that the examinations were behind her, that she had done well. She should have felt relieved and pleased. Instead, as the long day passed with Blanche taking Mary from supper to evening reading and study groups, Mary felt a growing dread.

Her sight had been gone for two years now, and Mary had always faced her affliction without outward complaint. Her life at home had gone on more or less as before, and she had gradually learned how to function there without sight. Mary knew she made things look easier than they really were, and she meant to. It had taken her ages to be able to get around her own house, to find things to cook or sew with. But Mary made sure no one knew how much she struggled, because she wanted to regain her independence as quickly as possible to avoid being a burden. And Laura was always nearby to help. When they moved from Minnesota to Dakota Territory, Laura had faithfully narrated the world to Mary, her words so vivid, it seemed that Mary's sightless eyes had actually seen every inch of their journey from Minnesota to Silver

Lake, and then on to De Smet. Laura and Carrie had taken the chores Mary could no longer do. Ma arranged the kitchen things in a special order so Mary would know where to find what she needed. And in truth, Mary had always preferred being indoors to out. She liked working with her hands and sewing, and she was still able to do that. What she missed most was being able to read, and to study and attend school. It had been especially hard to accept that she would now never become a teacher. Still, Mary had never yearned to travel and experience new things as Laura did. In the familiar confines of home, Mary had been very content.

And now all that had changed. Mary had accepted living without her sight, but now that she was here, she wasn't sure if she could accept living without her family for so much time. Mary had longed to attend this college ever since Reverend Alden had first told the Ingallses about it. But she hadn't realized what it would feel like to start alone in a strange place, learning to read and write and make her way around as if she were a little child. Was it worth it?

Stop it, Mary told herself. This is what I want. This is a good thing, and I am a very lucky girl.

Nonetheless, hot tears wetted Mary's eyes. Embarrassed, she wiped them away and sniffed as quietly as she could.

"Mary? Are you crying?" came Blanche's soft voice.

Mary had thought Blanche was still asleep.

"No, Blanche, I'm not crying," whispered Mary. "I didn't mean to wake you. I just have a tickle in my nose."

"Good night, then," Blanche said sleepily.

Mary Ingalls never wept and never lied. Here with Blanche, she had just done both. What was happening to her?

In the morning, the arrival of Hannah just before breakfast provided Mary with a welcome distraction from the bleak night before. Hannah burst through the door just as Mary and Blanche had finished washing up and were getting dressed. When Hannah started speaking, Mary thought she had never heard a person talk so fast.

"Here our new roommate arrives, and I've missed days! What a time to get sick! I thought my head would burst, it was so stuffed. Mary, how are you getting along? I'm Hannah, but you must know that. Have you taken the entrance examinations? Did your folks bring you—are they still in town? If Blanche kicks you or steals the covers, you can share a bed with me instead. Does she steal covers? I know she snores."

Mary felt as if Hannah had reached out and spun her around, leaving her dizzied and speechless.

"For heaven's sake, Hannah, slow down," cried Blanche. "And why do you always insist I snore?"

"Because you do," Hannah retorted. "Doesn't she, Mary? You can say. Blanche won't mind. Though maybe you've been too tired to notice—I was so tired my first week here, I slept through breakfast three times!"

"You've never missed a meal in your life, Hannah Ames," said Blanche, chuckling.

"Well, I *do* love to eat," Hannah replied, a laugh in her voice. "And there's nothing wrong with that."

Mary felt Hannah's arm reach around her waist. Mary was surprised, but she returned the hug, putting her arm around Hannah's solid frame.

"I'm sure we'd like to meet your folks, Mary, before they go," Blanche said.

"Oh, yes, we *must* meet them! What are they like? Do they have a long journey home? Are they worried about leaving you? My ma cried for days after first leaving me here. And I cried for days, too!"

"Hannah, do stop chattering," Blanche said. "The quarter bell has just rung. If we don't go down to breakfast now, we'll be late for chapel."

Hannah slipped her arm through Mary's.

"Then by all means, let's go!" Hannah said.

Mary smiled. She enjoyed Hannah's chattering and enthusiasm. It was a nice contrast to Blanche's quiet sweetness. She had been very lucky to get two such amiable roommates.

She already knew that it was forty-one steps from their bedroom door to the landing where the stairs began. Twenty-six steps down the second flight of stairs brought them to the main hall. The smell of breakfast and sound of voices gave Mary the direction of the dining hall, though Hannah was already pulling her that way.

Hannah continued her lively talking through breakfast, with an occasional amused admonishment from Blanche. Mary was relieved to simply be part of the audience. She answered Hannah's questions but found her mind wandering as her roommate chattered about people and places Mary was unfamiliar with. For some reason she didn't have much of an appetite that morning, and instead of eating, she used the sounds in the dining room to create a picture of the room in her head.

The ceilings were high, and judging by the warmth Mary occasionally felt when she turned her head, she could tell there were large windows on one wall with sunshine streaming in. Blanche had told her that students sat sixteen to a table, and from the voices on both sides, Mary guessed there were six tables in the room. The floor was wooden, and Mary could feel it vibrate when someone walked by or pushed back a chair.

Mary listened to how many different kinds of voices were blending together. Some were high and clearly pitched. Mary guessed they were girls, or maybe boys of seven or eight years old. To her left, she could hear controlled but regular eruptions of giggles that reminded her of Laura's laugh. And from across the room came the deeper tones of young men who might be her own age or older.

So many new people. Pa had told Mary there were ninety-six students attending the college. Mary wondered if she had known ninety-six people in the sum of her entire life. Would she ever know one voice from the other? Hannah and Blanche had introduced her to so many people. For the time being, her roommates' voices were the only ones she was sure she recognized. Hannah's voice was robust and deep, and Blanche's was quieter and more elegantly pitched.

"Don't you, Mary?" Hannah was asking. Mary did not realize Hannah had been talking to her.

"I'm sorry, Hannah," Mary said. "I was a bit lost in thought. I didn't hear you."

"I've never known anyone to say they had trouble hearing Hannah," came a voice from across the table.

That sounds like Charlotte, Mary thought. Blanche had said everyone sat at the same table each meal, in the same seats.

Hannah gave a good-natured laugh. "I was talking about hotcakes," she said. "They almost never make them here. I miss them. Don't you, Mary?"

"Yes," said Mary wistfully. "My Ma makes wonderful hotcakes."

As Mary thought about Ma's delicious hotcakes and syrup, a bell rang.

"There goes the bell for chapel, Hannah. You see, you've talked so much, you haven't finished your breakfast again," said Blanche wryly.

"Do we have to go outside to get to the

chapel?" Mary asked. "I haven't brought a wrap down with me."

Though Mary had been at the college for several days, she had not yet begun her full regular daily schedule. Chapel was offered twice every day, but today would be Mary's first time attending.

"The chapel is upstairs in the north wing," said Blanche. Mary heard her stand up. "We don't go out of doors to get there. But there will be time for a walk later, if you like."

"Blanche is a great one for walks," Hannah said, sounding less than enthusiastic about that activity.

Mary stood up and folded her napkin, placing it in her pocket. All around was the sound of chairs scraping back, and footsteps and voices moving toward the door.

"Hannah Ames—" Blanche began.

Mary heard the clink of a fork being dropped to the table, and a chair squeaking on the floorboards. Hannah must have been finishing up the breakfast she hadn't eaten because she'd been too busy talking.

"I'm ready, Blanche. I'm finished. I'm not going to make us late again."

"You always say that, but then you *do* make us late," Blanche said. But she didn't sound too upset.

Mary tried to resume her step counting as her roommates led her from the dining hall, but too many sounds and thoughts distracted her. She soon gave up. With chapel twice each day, Mary would learn the way there soon enough. For the moment, she gave herself over to Blanche's guiding arm, turning her face to catch the sunlight when they passed a window.

If Ma and Pa leave for home today, they'll have a fine day for traveling, Mary thought.

When the girls stepped through a doorway into a cool, quiet room, Mary knew that they were in the chapel. Their footsteps made echoes, and Mary pictured a long, deep room with high ceilings.

"We sit in the eighth pew from the back, on the right," Blanche whispered to Mary.

Mary reached out her right hand and felt the smooth varnished back of the first pew. She kept her hand out, lightly touching each pew until they came to the eighth. Hannah slid in first, followed by Blanche. Mary followed, sliding easily on the well-polished bench.

This was the first place Mary had come to since arriving in Vinton where she felt she knew exactly what to do and how to behave. The Ingallses had attended many different churches in all the places they had lived. Some had been held in the houses of homesteaders. In one town, they had gone to a church Pa helped build with his own hands. In other places they had gone to larger, older churches. But always, somehow, it felt the same. It was a comforting, familiar feeling that made Mary feel peaceful.

When the organ began, the students stood and Mary rose with them. She immediately recognized the hymn and joined in happily. It was one of Ma's favorites:

There is a happy land,
Far, far away,
Where saints in glory stand,
Bright, bright as day.

Later, there were several readings from the Bible, as well as a quiet prayer time and a short sermon. Mary tried to follow the sermon, but her mind kept wandering back to thoughts of Ma and Pa. The service closed with another hymn Mary knew well. As they were standing up to leave, Mary heard someone stop at the end of their pew.

"Mary?"

Mary recognized Miss Mattice's voice immediately.

"Hello, Miss Mattice," Mary said warmly.

"Good morning, Miss Mattice," Blanche said.

"Miss Mattice, don't you think Mary is settling in beautifully?" Hannah asked.

"She certainly is, Hannah. And good morning to you, too, Blanche. Mary, I wanted to let you know that you have passed your examinations and have ranked quite high. Your parents will be arriving at the school shortly. I'll take you to them."

Miss Mattice led Mary out of the chapel, and Blanche and Hannah walked beside them.

Mary was feeling so many different things at once, it made her dizzy. Blanche's hand rested lightly on Mary's shoulder as they walked.

"Mary, you've passed your examinations!" Hannah exclaimed. "Now you may pick your classes! You simply must take the organ—it is the best music class. And you will take sewing, won't you? And beadwork? And Miss Mattice, I think Mary ought to begin with our political economy class, don't you? That way we would all be taking the same classes. Blanche, wouldn't that be nice?"

"Slow down, Hannah," said Miss Mattice, a smile in her voice. "One thought at a time."

Miss Mattice pulled Mary a little closer and spoke softly to her.

"We are all very pleased with your work, Mary. Well done."

"Thank you, Miss Mattice," Mary said, her face flushing with pleasure.

"I sent a teacher's aide to take the good news to your parents at their hotel early this morning. Now that your enrollment here is official, Mary, they will need to make their way home to your family."

Mary knew this, of course, but her stomach tightened. Ma and Pa were leaving.

"We've made arrangements for our driver to take your parents to the train station to meet the nine o'clock. They're waiting downstairs to say good-bye."

Mary felt as if she were in a dream. She knew she must walk and talk, but she felt weighed down and fuzzy.

"Mary, can we come with you to meet your folks?" Hannah asked eagerly. "Who knows when we'll get the chance again? Miss Mattice, if Mary doesn't mind, may we?"

"Hannah," Blanche said, "Mary will want to be alone with her folks."

Mary hesitated. Part of her did want to be alone with Ma and Pa to say good-bye. It would be so long before she saw them again and it was going to be terribly hard having them go. On the other hand, Mary knew that her folks were probably sad too, and worrying. Ma would be wondering over and over if it was really the right thing, leaving Mary in Vinton.

If Blanche and Hannah were with her, and Ma could see how friendly and kind they were, perhaps it would make her feel better. And Hannah's eagerness to meet Ma and Pa warmed Mary's heart.

"I should like you both to come, if it is all right with Miss Mattice," Mary said.

Hannah gave a little squeal of satisfaction.

"Very well, then," Miss Mattice said. "All three of you may go. I have a teacher waiting for me in my office, so I will put you in charge, Blanche, and the three of you may go to the front entrance hallway together. Afterward, Blanche, please bring Mary to my office so that we may go over her curriculum. You and Hannah might be late to your second-period class, so I will give you a note for your teacher at that time."

"Yes, Miss Mattice," Blanche said.

Miss Mattice put her arms around Mary and hugged her.

"Welcome to the Iowa College for the Blind, Mary. I have a feeling we're going to be very proud of you."

"Thank you," Mary whispered.

Blanche and Hannah each took one of Mary's arms, and they set off down the hallway they had come through for chapel.

"We'll be taking the same staircase that goes to the dining hall level," Blanche explained as they walked. "Then we will head east, in the opposite direction we went for breakfast. Don't worry, I know it must seem confusing now. But the buildings and grounds are laid out very logically. You will have it sorted out in no time."

Blanche had slowed the pace suddenly, letting Mary know that they had come to the top of a staircase. The air was warmer, and Mary could sense that there was a large window facing the staircase landing. She made a picture of the stairs in her mind, envisioning each step, each landing and turn that lay ahead.

It was then that she fell. One moment she was lowering her foot to a step, and the next she felt her foot slip forward, her weight flying back. Mary came down heavily into a half-sitting, half-lying position, pulling Blanche down on one side of her and Hannah halfway down on the other.

Mary's back had come down hard on the edge of a step, and it hurt. The wind had been knocked out of her from the fall, and she tried to catch her breath. For a moment, all three girls were simply frozen in place.

"Oh, my," said Hannah, breaking the silence.

Mary felt Blanche, who was still holding her arm, begin to get to her feet. Mary stood up with her, though gingerly.

"Are you all right, Mary?" Blanche asked worriedly.

"I . . . yes, I'm all right. I'm so sorry! Are you all right, Blanche? Hannah?" Mary's voice shook a little. She'd thought she was paying enough attention, but she was wrong. Not only had she fallen, she had taken Blanche down with her. Falling down a staircase could be a very serious thing. Mary knew if Hannah had not been holding so tight and steady on her other side, the fall might have been much more serious.

"Oh, we're fine, Mary. Don't sound so

spooked," Hannah said. "Believe me, these things happen all the time. People walk into things or slip. So many feet go up and down these stairs, they are worn smooth as glass in some places. I think they ought to put a bit of rug down, but that muffles sound. Don't you find the sound of things helps you sort out where you are? Some of the older students say they can tell where they are in the hallway just by snapping their fingers as they walk and listening to the sound it makes. Never mind that they might feel silly walking down the hallway snapping away as if they're listening to a jig."

Mary was still shaken but couldn't help feeling reassured by Hannah. Whether Hannah sensed her conversation was helpful or was merely being her usual talkative self, she pressed right on with another story as they resumed walking down the stairs.

"I once toppled right off the steps we used for climbing into our buggy at home. I landed in a puddle and was soaked through and through, even down to my new gloves. I had to be taken straight back inside to get some dry things, so we missed the church service we were going to, and I wasn't even scolded because it wasn't my fault. The steps had iced over."

They had come to the bottom of the stairs. Mary still found herself unable to think of anything to say. Blanche leaned closer to her for a moment.

"Mary, we have all fallen," she said softly. "Miss Mattice says it is not the way you fall, but the way you get to your feet again that shows the kind of person you are."

Blanche knew Mary had not brushed the fall off as easily and cheerfully as had Hannah.

"Thank you, Blanche," Mary said as they rounded a corner. The cooler air of the front entrance hall reached Mary's face.

"Mary!" came a voice.

"Ma!" Mary called in the direction of the voice. She wanted to rush to Ma, but she did not want to risk losing her footing again. It was important that she appear happy and adjusted to college during this last time with her parents. Thank goodness they had not seen her fall!

Ma and Pa came to her, and Ma's arms

wrapped around her in a hug. She could smell the comforting and familiar scent of Pa's pipe tobacco faintly in the air. Mary heard a little sniff from Hannah.

"Ma, Pa, these are my roommates, Blanche and Hannah."

"I'm pleased to meet you, Mr. and Mrs. Ingalls," Blanche said. "We're so happy to have Mary in our room."

"It is lovely to meet you both," Ma said. "How long have you been attending college?"

"I'm in my second year," Hannah said eagerly. "But Blanche is an old hand. She is in her third."

"It's kind of you both to come down to meet us," Pa said. "Now we will be able to tell Mary's sisters who she is living with. As you can imagine, they will be full of questions."

"Please let them know Mary has settled in very nicely," Blanche said. "She will be well looked after here. We'll make certain of that."

"I'm sure you will," said Ma in her warmest voice. "It does me good knowing Mary is living with such kind and generous girls."

Mary smiled. This was exactly what she

had hoped Ma would feel if she met Blanche and Hannah.

"I'm going to be very happy, Ma," Mary said, "though I shall miss my family every minute."

"I wish that we could bring you home for Christmas, Mary," Pa said. "But I'm afraid we just can't manage it this year."

"I understand, Pa," Mary said. "I don't mind so much."

But Mary did mind. She adored Christmas at home. There were so many things to look forward to—Ma's special meals, and the gathering of family. The squeals of delight from Carrie and Grace on Christmas morning, when every table setting had a gift in front of it. Ma's brown-sugar Christmas cakes, and her baked sweet potatoes. Carrie and Grace making paper dolls. Her family would send her letters, of course, and no doubt Laura would describe every single moment of their holiday. But that would not make up for missing the sounds, the smells, and the feeling of excitement.

"Mary will be able to write to you soon," Hannah said. "She will be learning to read

Braille, of course, but she will also learn to write letters that you can read. We each have a special slate with grooves. It's called a handwriting guide, and Mary can learn to write out whole letters by hand."

"How wonderful," Ma said. "I hadn't thought Mary would be able to write to us herself."

"I will write as soon as I have learned to use the guide," Mary promised.

"And we will write you each week," Ma said. "Miss Mattice told us that there is always someone available to read students their letters from home."

"Oh, it's true. It's always such a wonderful thing to hear a letter," Hannah exclaimed.

A pause followed. Mary shifted uncomfortably in the silence.

"I expect we ought to get moving along if we aim to catch that train," Pa said. Mary noticed that his voice sounded funny.

Pa put his arms around Mary, and she stepped up on her tiptoes and hugged him back, breathing in all of him, savoring the soft lapel of his coat and the prickle of his beard.

"Good-bye, Pa," Mary said, swallowing hard.

Then it was Ma's turn.

She hugged Mary so tight, Mary thought the breath might go out of her. And still it did not seem tight enough.

"I am so proud of you, Mary," Ma said. "You will be getting such a good education. It is such a blessing, and after you have waited so long. Remember that we will be thinking of you every day, and praying for you. We will have patience, because we know that you will be coming back to us."

"Yes, Ma," Mary said. She wanted to say much more, to agree that she was blessed and that she intended to excel at college. She wanted to thank her parents one more time for everything they had sacrificed to send her here.

But Mary did not trust her voice. And she did not want Ma and Pa's last picture of her to be of her in tears.

"Good-bye, Ma. Good-bye, Pa," she half whispered.

"Good-bye, Mary," Pa said. Mary could tell he was already turning toward the door. She knew that he had been dreading this moment.

"Good-bye, Mary," Ma said, giving Mary's arm a little rub. "My good girl."

Then the loving, warm pressure of Ma's hand on Mary's arm was gone, and Mary could hear the sound of the great wooden front door opening and closing again.

Ma and Pa were gone. She was alone.

Beside her, Hannah gave a great sob.

"Hannah Ames!" cried Blanche. "Shame on you!"

"I can't help it," Hannah said between deep, weepy breaths. "I hate good-byes!"

"But this isn't *your* good-bye, it's Mary's!" Blanche retorted. "And she is managing to keep herself composed, isn't she?"

"Mary," Hannah sniffed, "do you forgive me?"

Hannah sounded so theatrical that Mary almost laughed out loud. And she was truly grateful for the diversion. Mary reached out a hand.

"Where are you?" she asked. Then she felt Hannah's hand slip into hers.

"Here I am."

"I'm glad you came to meet my folks," Mary said. "Both of you."

"They're lovely, Mary," Blanche said. "I do know how much you'll miss them. But you *will* have fun here too. I promise. Now we must get you to Miss Mattice's office, so Hannah and I can get to class."

"Oh, there's no need to rush, is there?" Hannah asked. "After all, no one else knows the Ingallses have just left. For all anybody knows, they might stand around here another ten minutes talking."

"We *do* need to rush," Blanche said firmly. "You may not care how much of the class you miss, but I do. Come on, Mary."

Mary let her roommates take her arms, Blanche on the left and Hannah on the right, as she was becoming accustomed to.

It felt good to be surrounded by people she could trust.

Daisy Chain

Mary had enrolled in higher mathematics, political economy, English literature, sewing, knitting, and beadwork. Best of all, she was to take organ lessons. Mary had always longed to take music lessons, perhaps even learn to play duets with Pa on his fiddle, but there had never been money for such an extravagance, and the Ingallses could not afford to buy a piano or an organ. Now she would be learning to play the organ as part of her schoolwork. It was almost too good to be true.

Mary's first class today was to be beadwork. The morning had already passed, what with saying good-bye to Ma and Pa and working out her schedule with Miss Mattice. So Mary had missed several classes already. She would have to begin them tomorrow morning.

As Hannah had hoped, Mary found that one or both of her roommates were in most of the classes she had chosen. But neither one of them was taking beadwork. Someone else from that class would come to take Mary to the classroom. Once again, Mary found herself sitting on her bed, waiting. Her stomach growled, and she wished now that she had not skipped lunch. But when Mary felt nervous, she lost her appetite.

The bell signaling the end of lunch rang. There would be ten minutes, Mary knew, before the next bell rang for the beginning of the first afternoon class period. She listened to the muffled swell of sound as students poured out of the dining hall downstairs and made their way to their next classes. So many students. So many classrooms. How did they all manage without colliding into one another?

Though there had been no knock, the door

to Mary's room squeaked open. Mary got expectantly to her feet, listening.

"Hello?" Mary asked after a moment.

"Don't be all day about it," a voice retorted. "I'm going to be late already, burdened with the likes of you."

Mary's heart sank. It was Mattie who would take Mary to beadwork. This was not exactly an ideal way to begin her first college class.

"I'm ready," Mary said.

"Then what are you standing around for?" Mattie asked.

"I'm waiting for you to guide me to the class," Mary said, sounding more impatient than she had intended. But really, how exasperating. Mattie knew she had been sent to show Mary to the classroom. She knew perfectly well Mary could not see to follow her down the hall.

Mattie sighed heavily, and Mary felt her arm taken, none too gently.

"Come along, then, Miss Good Girl," Mattie said. "Or would you rather I carried you on my back?"

Mary had a good mind to say what she'd

really rather Mattie do, but she kept the thought to herself, though her face burned with anger.

They walked down the hallway, Mary mentally counting the steps until they reached the stairs. She knew this part, now. She could get from her room to the stairs alone. As they reached the staircase, Mary could feel the space opening up. Sounds disappeared into the largeness. Mary envisioned the steps before her, her back still smarting from the morning's fall. Cautiously, she held back as Mattie began down the stairs. Mary would not take the first step until she had the banister grasped firmly in her hand.

"The stairs don't move by themselves," Mattie snapped. "If you want to get to the bottom, you actually have to *walk*!"

"I know that," Mary said in a low voice. But she was not about to tell Mattie she had fallen earlier. "I'm only being careful."

"'I'm only being careful,'" Mattie said, imitating Mary's clear voice.

It was becoming apparent that this girl was

even meaner than Laura and Mary's old enemy Nellie Oleson. There was an anger that simmered in Mattie all the time. Mary had never known such a hostile person in her entire life.

They made their way down two flights of stairs in silence. Mattie had a tight and uncomfortable hold on Mary's arm now, and she half led, half pulled Mary along. Unlike her roommates, Mattie didn't explain anything about the direction they were going.

As soon as I get the chance, Mary thought, I will ask Blanche to teach me the way to the beadwork room. I will make sure I never need Mattie's help again.

"Here," Mattie said suddenly, and her hand was gone from Mary's arm.

What did "here" mean? Where had Mattie left her? Mary stood for a moment, trying to sort out where she was through the sounds. She guessed she was still standing in the corridor. She reached out with her right hand and brushed a wooden doorjamb with her fingertips. This must be the door to the beadwork room, and Mattie had simply left her right outside it.

Mary felt a light touch on her back.

"Oh, excuse me," a girl said, her voice coming from behind Mary. "Are you going inside?"

Mary recognized Charlotte's voice, to her great relief.

"You're Charlotte, aren't you?" Mary asked.

"Yes. Hello, Mary Ingalls," Charlotte replied. "Are you taking beadwork?"

"Yes, I am. Is this the right room?"

"It is indeed," Charlotte replied. "Come on inside with me. We can find seats together."

Mary gratefully followed Charlotte into the classroom. She could hear perhaps five or six voices talking. Miss Mattice had told her there would be nine students in this class.

"I usually sit nearest the door," Charlotte said, "but I think there are two open seats together across the room. Let's sit there."

"I'd like that," Mary said. She hoped Mattie's seat was nowhere nearby.

Mary could tell from the direction of voices that the seats were arranged in a large circle.

"Here is your seat, Mary," Charlotte said. "Slide in from the side, because there is an arm with a table attached."

Mary ran her hand over the back of the seat and side table, then sat down.

"Why, it's warmer on this side of the room," Charlotte exclaimed. "You've done me a favor, Mary. I'm always chilled to the bone, and this is a nice warm seat."

"Good afternoon, all," came a woman's voice before Mary could reply to Charlotte. The chattering around the classroom ceased.

"Good morning, Miss Hennick," the class responded.

Mary wondered what Miss Hennick looked like, and whether she could see. She knew that some of the teachers at the college were blind, or only partially sighted. But I imagine Miss Hennick can see, Mary thought. How else could she teach beadwork?

"We have a new student with us this morning," said Miss Hennick. From her voice, Mary guessed that she was an older woman. "Mary Ingalls comes to us from De Smet, in Dakota Territory. Please extend her a nice welcome."

"Welcome, Mary," came a number of voices

together. Mary did not hear Mattie's voice among them. She had not heard Mattie at all since Charlotte had brought her in from the hallway. Was she even here?

"I'm going to be handing out the pieces you have all been working on," Miss Hennick said briskly. "Please continue with your work, so that I may have some time to go over a stitch with Mary."

Mary heard rustling, feet and bodies shifting, and some quiet talking.

"Do you like to sew, Mary?" Charlotte asked.

"Oh, I love to," Mary replied. "Even now it still comes easily to me. My sister Laura says I can see with my fingers when I sew."

"You said at breakfast the other day that you went blind from scarlet fever, didn't you?" Charlotte asked.

"Yes, two years ago."

Mary still wasn't used to people asking her so openly how she had gone blind, but she found it was getting easier to talk about it. She was beginning to sense that having no eyesight bonded the students here together. At home, being blind had always made Mary feel different, but here it made her feel that she belonged.

"Here is your piece, Charlotte," came Miss Hennick's voice.

"Thank you, Miss," replied Charlotte.

Mary heard the sound of a chair being pulled up next to her.

"Mary," Miss Hennick began, "let me tell you a little about what we do here. Of course, most of your learning at the beginning will have to take place by trial and error."

"Yes, Miss," Mary said. She suppressed a feeling of excitement. This was her very first class. Her new education had officially begun.

"First, I want to stress that we do not teach beadwork simply as a way to keep you occupied later in life. Beadwork can be used to make many beautiful things, such as handbags or jewelry, which students can give as gifts or even sell for money."

Mary nodded seriously.

"I'm placing a box on the table in front of you," said Miss Hennick. She took Mary's hand and guided it over the box, which was divided into small partitions.

"On the side of the box closest to you, there are compartments for needles on the left, thread in the middle, and clasps on the right. You will find the scissors here, on a ribbon. I recommend you wear them around your neck during class."

Mary took the scissors and put the ribbon over her head as if it were a necklace.

Miss Hennick moved Mary's hand to the next row.

"Here are your beads," she said. "They come in many different shapes and colors, but to begin with, I will start you with some fairly large beads. There is a slot in each compartment where we place Braille labels that tell what color bead is there. But since you have not yet learned to read Braille, I have filled only three compartments, with blue, red, and white beads. You can remember which are which because I have put them in alphabetical order from left to right."

Mary reached into the compartments, feeling the cluster of beads in each one. Blue, red, and white. Miss Hennick was right—that was easy to remember.

"I'm going to have you begin by learning the daisy chain stitch. Most beginners find that it is easy to learn, and it is a very pretty stitch. Give me your hand, please, Mary," Miss Hennick said.

Mary felt her teacher place a small beaded object into her hand.

"This is a bracelet made with the daisy chain stitch," Miss Hennick explained. "Tell me what you think it looks like."

Mary ran her fingers over the bracelet. She could tell immediately that it was made of linked circles. Touching each link, she could feel a larger bead in the center of its circle.

"It is in little round flower shapes," Mary said, "with a larger bead in the center. Each flower is linked to the next, like a real daisy chain."

"Very good, Mary," said her teacher. "Anything else? What colors do you think it might have?"

How was Mary supposed to tell that? But

she thought for a moment, making what her fingers had felt into a picture that her mind could examine. To her surprise, the picture did include colors.

"I would guess that the beads that make up each circle are a light color, and the larger bead in the center is dark. That would make the flower shapes look like daisies. If I were using the beads that I have, I might use white on the outside and red in the middle."

"Excellent," Miss Hennick said, pleasure evident in her voice. "You have a very good feel for this, Mary. I want you to study this bracelet awhile, and get used to the feel of your own beads and thread. Will you need help threading a needle?"

"Oh, no, Miss," replied Mary. "I do . . . I mean I *did* quite a bit of sewing at home."

"Good. When you are ready, then, thread the needle, knot one end of the thread, and practice pulling beads down onto the thread. Use different colors, and try to keep track of what colors are where."

"Yes, Miss Hennick," Mary replied.

Mary had already memorized where everything in her box was. She unraveled some thread, cut one end, and knotted it. Mary chose a medium-sized needle and threaded it on her first try. She smiled, remembering how Laura had always begged Mary to thread her needles for her, because she was so good at it.

Mary began threading the beads easily, alternating her pattern of blue, red, and then white. As she worked, she thought about the Osage beads she and Laura had found with Pa at an abandoned campsite on the prairie so many years ago. They had crawled over the grass for hours collecting the beads, and had strung them into a necklace for Carrie, then just a baby. The memory made time pass quickly, and Mary had just used her last bead when she heard Miss Hennick's footsteps approaching.

"I can see you are going to be a quick study," the teacher said. "I think you are ready to learn the daisy chain stitch. Unstring those beads, and I'll explain how to begin. It usually takes several tries even if you are already skilled at sewing, so don't expect it to be perfect the first time."

Mary listened carefully as Miss Hennick gave her each step to make the pattern. She found she could anticipate some of the moves before her teacher described them.

"I know that was a lot of information," Miss Hennick said. "But I'd like you to work by yourself for a while and try to get a start on the chain. Do you have any questions?"

"No, Miss," Mary replied. She was eager to start, her fingers itching to make the flower-shaped pattern. She waited until Miss Hennick had walked away to help another student. Then she began. Thread five beads, loop back through the first. Thread three beads and loop back. Thread one. Loop back. Thread one again. Loop back. Thread four and loop. Now three and loop.

Mary ran her fingers over her work and almost laughed out loud with pleasure. She knew without being told that she had made two perfect flowers in her daisy chain. Mary lost all sense of time as she worked to make a third, then a fourth. She was finishing her seventh flower when the bell rang.

"Students, put your things away, please," came Miss Hennick's voice. Mary heard her approaching.

"Now Mary, why don't we—" Miss Hennick stopped suddenly. Mary felt her take the daisy chain from her hand.

"My heavens!" her teacher exclaimed. "This is beautiful work, Mary. I don't know of any new student I've had who could do this on the first try. Have you worked with beads before?"

"No, Miss," Mary replied, feeling her face flush with pleasure and a little bit of embarrassment at the compliment. "I have made lace, though."

"Well, this is very good work indeed," her teacher said. "Well done, Mary."

"Thank you, Miss Hennick," Mary said.

Miss Hennick began speaking to another student. Mary felt a hand on her arm. She had been so consumed with her daisy chain,

Mary had forgotten Charlotte was sitting in the next seat.

"Good for you!" Charlotte said. "It took me ages and ages to get the hang of beading when I began. Miss Hennick does not give praise lightly. When she says 'well done,' you know you must really be good!"

"I know something else Mary Ingalls is good at," came Mattie's voice. So she *was* there in the classroom. Why had she been so silent up until now? "Can you guess what I mean, Mary?" Mattie taunted. She kept her voice low, probably hoping the teacher would not overhear her.

"Whatever you mean, I'm sure it isn't nice," Charlotte said. She stood up, her hand still on Mary's arm.

"Well, go ahead and tell us, then," came a girl's voice that Mary did not recognize.

"She is good at dropping them all over the floor," Mattie said. "She uses the Clumsy Oaf stitch."

Mary's face flushed with anger as she heard

someone laughing. Was the laughter directed at Mary?

"Mattie," came Miss Hennick's sharp voice. "That will be quite enough."

Mary ducked her head. Had *everyone* heard? I hate Mattie, Mary thought furiously. I know it is wrong, but I do. I hate her.

WORD FROM HOME

Mary was still smarting from Mattie's words during the reading and study period before bed that night. Miss Mattice had come up to the study hall to check on how Mary was doing. She had brought Mary a handwriting guide and suggested she practice using it.

The guide was the size of a sheet of writing paper, and it had long slots, one on top of the other, like lines on a page. Mary was to press the paper into the grooved slots, then follow with her fingers as she wrote her letters in the indentations. Mary kept her left finger lightly touching the tip of the pencil, so when she finished one letter, her finger would cover it and she would move the pencil to the right to begin the next letter. Between words, Mary learned, she was to use a space of one finger width. The slots would keep each line straight, and Mary would know when she had finished one line and needed to go on to the next.

Mary sat at a desk in the study hall, the writing guide in front of her. A fire crackled in the hearth at one end of the room. Mary usually loved nothing better than the smoky scent of a fire, but this evening she barely noticed it. She held a pencil in one hand but was not writing. She felt exhausted. Every time Mary thought she was settling in, something happened. She thought she was doing well, then she fell on the stairs. She'd been feeling badly, then Miss Hennick had praised her beadwork. That had made her happy until Mattie's taunting had made Mary unhappy all over again.

Now Mary could not stop thinking about

Laura. With each hour that passed, Mary missed her sister more. Mary had always been the sister with the best manners, the girl who never spoke sharply or out of turn. Laura, on the other hand, had never stood idly by while any member of her family was treated badly.

Laura always told Mary how she admired her good behavior. Did she know how much Mary admired Laura's spunk? It was easy to be a good, well-mannered girl when one had a sister like Laura. All Mary ever had to do was hold her tongue and hide her feelings, and Laura would jump in. Laura was always quick to speak up and was always the one punished for it. Mary was not really a good girl. She had just never learned how to stand up for herself as Laura did.

What would Laura have done if someone had poked fun at her in front of a class, or if she had heard some of the things Mattie had said to Mary?

Mary realized she was gripping the pencil so hard, her fingers hurt. I must pull myself together, she told herself. I am supposed to be practicing my writing. Mary felt for the first grooved line on the handwriting guide, and began to write.

Dear Laura,

I am finally here at college, thanks to you and Ma and Pa. I know how hard you all worked so that I could be here.

I am happy, of course. But Laura, I did not realize how dreadfully I would miss you, how much it would hurt. You have always thought me such a good girl, but that isn't quite true. I only seemed good because you were always brave and outspoken enough for both of us. Now you are not here, and I must learn to stand up for myself.

There is a vicious girl here who has taken a terrible dislike to me. She says cruel things, and I say nothing to defend myself. I think you would be ashamed of my silence, Laura. If you were here, I wouldn't mind this girl. I always feel

strong with you. But now I am not so
sure I can do this alone. I will never feel
at home here, I will never—

Mary stood up abruptly, removing the paper from the writing guide. She turned toward the fireplace and listened for the sounds of voices, the scratches of pencils, and the turning of pages until she could picture the positions of the other desks. With one hand extended in front of her, she walked toward the fireplace. When her hand grew hot, Mary knew she was almost directly in front of the fire. With one quick gesture, Mary tossed her crumpled letter over the screen and into the fire, listening to the satisfying little hiss of it being burned to ash.

It was all right, she thought. She hadn't meant to send the letter. She was only practicing writing with the guide. And even though her words were now only soot in the hearth, Mary almost felt that she'd had a real conversation with Laura. Don't be silly, Laura would tell her. You are as brave as I am. You don't need me to be with you. You can take care of yourself—you are already doing it.

Laura's reassuring voice in Mary's head was as clear as a bell. By the time the study period was over and the fire was going out, Mary felt determined not to let Mattie get the better of her again.

Now that she was taking classes, Mary found that the days passed quickly. Every hour was tightly packed. The rising bell tolled at six o'clock, and Mary had only half an hour to wash up, dress, and help Blanche make the bed before going down to breakfast. Each morning all students attended the first session of chapel at seven fifteen, and academic classes began at seven forty-five. Students were given forty-five minutes for lunch at twelve fifteen, followed by afternoon sessions of industrial training and music lessons.

Mary especially looked forward to her organ lessons. Her teacher, Mr. Locke, told Mary that her organ lessons were as important as anything else she learned at college, and that she was an especially promising musician. Gifted students could find work as church organists, and some even went on to become music teachers themselves. The possibility that Mary might become a teacher after all made her passionately devoted to her lessons. At the moment, she was learning to play by ear, which meant listening to Mr. Locke play a phrase and then repeating it herself, through trial and error, until it was right. But Mr. Locke explained that as Mary learned to read Braille, she would also learn to read Braille-notated music. Then she would be able to learn and play new pieces almost as a sighted musician could.

After her organ lesson each day, there was an indoor recreation period. Each day also included scheduled free time. Mary had heard many of the girls enthusiastically describe the walking paths on the college grounds. But Mary had not yet been on a walk outside. Two days after Ma and Pa left, it had begun to rain. It had been raining on and off ever since, for six days.

It was a Friday evening, and the students were allowed to socialize as they pleased during the evening study period. The air was damp and cold, but as usual the study hall was cheery and cozy, heated by the large fire in the hearth.

Blanche, Hannah, and Mary had found some seats not too far from the fire. The oldest students had their pick of the warmest seats. But Mary was comfortable in the seat she had chosen, lulled by the fire and the pleasant chatter of her roommates. Blanche wanted to work on some lace, and Hannah was tackling a particularly tricky knitting project. Mary had a Braille reader in her lap. Everyone, including Mary's teachers, had told her that learning to read Braille might seem impossible at first. Mary was inclined to agree.

The open book on her lap was made up of rows and rows of raised dots arranged in lines. Each letter of the alphabet had a corresponding letter in Braille. The letter A, the first Mary learned, was represented in Braille by a single raised dot. The letter L was made by three dots in a vertical line. There were also Braille characters for numbers and punctuation marks, but Mary had not learned them yet.

Miss Mattice had told Mary she should consider Braille a whole new language, and that it took great patience to learn an entirely unfamiliar alphabet. Mary was working on memorizing the Braille character for each letter from the large practice alphabet in her reader. Miss Mattice had also brought Mary a Braille slate and stylus. The slate was made of two connected pieces of metal, one that created a solid surface for the paper, and one that lay atop the paper and was the actual guide. The top piece had four rectangular cutouts, alllowing the writer to create four lines of text. Within each rectangular cutout there were six grooves, one in each of the places a Braille dot might be. The stylus was used to punch indentations into the paper, which resulted in raised dots when the paper was turned over. Mary was learning both to read Braille by feel and to write in Braille with the slate and stylus. She would continue to use her handwriting guide to write out letters for her sighted friends and family back home.

"I didn't get nearly enough to eat at supper,

did you?" Hannah was asking. "Why, at home Ma serves nearly twice as much to my brothers and sisters."

"And is it possible your brothers and sisters are twice as large as most people?" Blanche asked with a laugh.

"Oh, there's no doubt about that," Hannah replied good-naturedly. "Pa says we are as solid a lot as Iowa has ever seen. I'm already dreaming about our Christmas supper. Ma cooks an enormous goose and makes mountains of biscuits and mashed potatoes and cranberry sauce, and oh, the pies!"

"Hannah, remember that Mary isn't able to go home for Christmas this year. Let's not make her feel bad about it with all this talk about your Christmas supper," Blanche said.

"Oh, I'm sorry, I'd forgotten!" Hannah exclaimed. "But surely there must be some way for you to go, isn't there, Mary? Maybe your folks will surprise you and—"

"Hannah!" Blanche said reproachfully. "Not every family is as fortunate as yours. You know that attending college is expensive, and so is traveling. My family lives very close by," Blanche explained to Mary. "So I am often able to find a ride and go home for the holidays."

"I didn't mean to sound unfeeling," Hannah said earnestly. "I'm sorry, Mary. I am always saying foolish things. But Mary, why not come spend Christmas with my family? My folks would love to have you. They would give you the train ticket, so you wouldn't have to spend a thing."

For a moment, Mary's heart leaped. How wonderful it would be to spend Christmas in someone's home, with delicious food and cheer. But Ma and Pa would not like Mary to take money from strangers for a train ticket.

"Thank you, Hannah. It's very nice of you, but Miss Mattice says there will be many students staying here for the holidays. I'll use the time to work on my Braille, so that I am reading as quickly as the rest of you when you return."

"I've stayed over before," Blanche said. "Last year, when my sister had the measles. There was a lot of quiet time with no chores to do. The Christmas meal was quite pleasant.

We all even got bags of Christmas candy from Miss Mattice."

"That does sound nice," Mary said. Of course it was nowhere near as nice as going home to her family, but it was getting easier to think of the college as a second home. On Christmas Day, however, Mary imagined, it would be very difficult not to feel glum.

"Tell me about your families," Mary said, partly to get her mind off her own family.

"There isn't much to tell about mine," Blanche said with a smile in her voice. "I'm not like Hannah and her army of brothers and sisters. There is just myself and my sister, Tillie. My pa owns a dry goods store. My ma is quite a good pianist. I expect you'd have a lot to talk about, since you both love music so. It's a quiet family, but a good and caring one, and I love them."

"My family is anything but quiet," Hannah said. "There are nine of us children, five boys and four girls. And we always have an assortment of cats and dogs. If the dogs and cats aren't fighting, some of my brothers and sisters are. When I first came to college, I could

hardly get used to it—I had never lived anywhere that wasn't noisy all the time! But you
have to speak up loudly in my house, or you
don't get your fair share. My brother Robert
will take food right off my plate if I don't pay
attention. Maybe that's why I'm always hungry.
We had a dog once that was always hungry, no
matter how much he ate. He was a terrier
named Pippa, and when he couldn't find any
food to steal, he'd take mittens and scarves and
sometimes socks and chew them up, then bury
the bits outside by the woodpile!"

Mary listened with a small smile on her face
as she traced her fingers over the alphabet. A,
one dot. That one was easy. B, two dots, one
above the other. C. Again two dots, but these
were side by side. I am sixteen years old, Mary
thought, and I am learning my ABC's. Laura
would think it funny that I am studying my
letters all over again.

Mary reviewed the first seven letters of the
alphabet, then practiced punching them onto
the paper with her slate and stylus.

"Blanche?" Mary asked. "I have made my

Braille letters through G. Would you check them and tell me if I have made any mistakes?"

"Of course," said Blanche. Mary placed the slate in Blanche's lap.

"I can check them too, Mary. My Braille is every bit as good as Blanche's. Now where was I in my story? Oh yes. Pippa had gone in and taken the matching sock from the drawer! He buried both of them neat as you please. My pa never even got the chance to wear them once! He wanted Ma to give Pippa away after that, but of course she didn't. We all would have raised a tremendous ruckus."

"We had a dog," Mary said wistfully. "A brindle bulldog named Jack."

"Did he take things like Pippa?" Hannah asked.

"No," Mary said. "He was brave and smart. Jack was a fine watchdog. If Pa had to travel, he said he always felt better knowing Jack was guarding us."

"He sounds like a wonderful dog, Mary," said Blanche. "Now, your letters are quite good, but you have mixed up your D with your F."

Mary sighed. So many people had told her Braille was difficult to learn, but secretly she had hoped she would have the same knack for it as beading and get it right immediately.

"They are easy to mix up," Blanche said. "They are the same shape, just pointing in opposite directions."

"Wait until you get to S and T," Hannah said. "It took me weeks to get them straight."

Weeks? Mary felt even more dejected. How could anyone stand to spend weeks learning two little letters?

"I have a feeling that Mary will study a good deal harder at her Braille than you did at first, Hannah. Don't you remember? You could scarcely keep at it for an hour before you would get tired of it and give up."

"I hated it," Hannah declared.

"I don't much care for it either," Mary said. "But I do love to read. That will make it all worthwhile."

Footsteps sounded, coming into the hall. To Mary's surprise, she heard her name.

"Mary Ingalls?" called a boy's voice.

"Put your hand up," said Blanche softly. "He can see you. That's Ben, one of the teaching assistants."

Mary raised her hand nervously. She didn't understand why a teacher's assistant would be looking for her. Could she have done something wrong? Or worse, was there bad news?

"Hello, Mary," the boy said. "I am Ben Holden. Miss Mattice asked me to bring you this letter. Usually we bring students their mail during recreation time, but Miss Mattice noticed it was a letter from home. Since you are so new here, she thought you might like to have it right away."

"Oh," Mary said. "That was awfully thoughtful of Miss Mattice."

Mary was surprised and curious at Ben's announcement. She wasn't expecting a letter from Ma and Pa so soon. Perhaps it was from Laura. But how could she read it?

"I'll be happy to read it to you," Ben said. "That's one of the things I do to help out. Or if you prefer, Miss Mattice could read it for you tomorrow at breakfast. The letter is from a Laura Ingalls."

It *was* from Laura! Mary did not think she could wait until morning for the letter. But it seemed improper to have a stranger read her personal letter. And not just a stranger, but a boy!

"I . . . I don't want to be any trouble . . . ," Mary stammered.

"It's no trouble, Miss," said Ben. "I don't mind either way."

Mary felt Blanche's hand on her arm, drawing Mary close.

"Mary, I can guess what you might be feeling," Blanche whispered. "It can be strange at first, to have your letters read out loud by someone else. Especially someone you haven't met until this moment. But you want your letter, and Ben can read it to you. It's one of the ways in which we all need help. I don't know anyone whose folks have learned to write in Braille."

Blanche was right. Though she would have preferred to have the letter read by Miss Mattice, it made no sense to wait. Mary hoped to get many letters from her family, and Miss Mattice would not always be around.

"Thank you, Ben," Mary said. "I would like to hear the letter, please."

"Mary will want some privacy," Blanche said. Mary heard her stand.

"Oh, no, you don't need to go," Mary said. "Really. You've met my parents. Now you can meet my sister, in a way."

"Good," said Hannah, happily. "I love letters. I don't care if they're for me or not!"

Mary heard the envelope being opened. She leaned forward expectantly, already forgetting her discomfort as Ben began to read.

Dear Mary,

You and Ma and Pa only left this morning, and it is already so strange in the house without you! I don't have time to write a proper letter yet, but Carrie thought it would be wonderful if we could mail you something right away, so you would have a letter as soon as possible. I imagine you'll agree that was a good idea.

We are planning a big surprise for Ma and Pa. Carrie and I have decided to do the fall housecleaning for Ma! We began as soon as you all left for the train station. We have washed the quilts and filled the straw ticks in each bed with fresh hay. It is wonderful to sleep on them, because now they smell like a summer day. We have scrubbed the floors, and we are working on washing the windows. Then we will iron the curtains. Grace is even going to blacken the stove, but we will watch her very carefully. The stove black makes such a mess if it is spilled. My hands ache dreadfully, but it will be such a great surprise! I can't wait to see Ma's face when she comes home and finds all the work done.

I know there must be times you feel lonely, Mary. I know I do now that you

are gone. But the time will pass quickly,
and before we know it, you will be home
again. I am glad you will be learning
so many new things, but part of me is
selfish and wishes you were with me. I
am so proud of you.

I will write again soon.

Love always,
Laura

A silence followed when Ben finished reading the letter. Mary still leaned forward in her chair, as if there might be more.

"Would you like me to read it again?" Ben asked. "I'd be happy to."

If Mary had been able, she would have read the letter over and over again, savoring each sentence. But she wouldn't ask Ben to do that. Mary felt as if she knew half the letter by heart already anyway.

"No thank you, Ben," Mary said. "You were very kind to bring me the letter."

"I'll leave it with you, then," Ben said.

He pressed the letter into Mary's hands, and

she ran her fingers over the envelope, tracing the raised square edges of the stamp.

"You all have a nice evening," Ben said.

"Thank you," Mary, Blanche, and Hannah replied in unison. Mary held the letter to her cheek as the footsteps faded. It even smelled like home.

"That was such a nice letter," Blanche said. "It must feel good to hear from your sister so soon."

"Oh, it does," Mary exclaimed. "Honestly, I feel as if she were just here, in this room."

"Imagine going home and finding all that housework done," Hannah said. "My brothers and sisters would never dream of doing such a thing, I can guarantee you. If they were home alone for the better part of a week, they would use the time to skip their baths, swim in their clothes, and eat every spoonful of sugar they could find."

Mary laughed out loud at the thought of Hannah's unruly siblings.

"What are your sisters like, Mary?" Hannah asked. "There are three of them, aren't there? Are they all like you, or are they very different?"

"Oh, I think they're different, each from the other," Mary said enthusiastically. "Laura is smart as a whip and absolutely fearless. Pa says she's as strong as a pony, too. She has always been my best friend, ever since we could both talk. Carrie is several years younger, and though she is also an excellent student, she is quite shy. Grace is still a baby, really, just four years old. She's good-natured and so pretty. I love them all, but I am closest to Laura. Just a little while ago I was imagining Laura was here talking with me."

"They all sound lovely," Hannah declared. "I am closest to one of my sisters, but some of my brothers can be absolute ruffians. One time when he was seven, Frederick collected an entire pail of snails and put them under my bedcovers, right where my feet went!"

Mary laughed as Hannah continued to regale them with stories of her siblings, though periodically her mind wandered to all the things she needed to do. She had to do better with her Braille and handwriting, and must work on her first organ piece. There was a political economy lesson to go over with Blanche and Hannah's help. There was more than enough to keep Mary very busy, and to keep her mind off home.

And for the moment, sitting by the fire with her new friends, Mary felt content.

THE STORM

The weather had been bad for such a
lengthy spell, Mary longed to take a
simple walk and feel a breeze on her face.
Finally there came an opportunity. It was
Sunday afternoon, lunch and chapel were over,
and there was a free hour before study time.

I could have a walk now, Mary thought,
even though the sun isn't out. It has stopped
raining, and that is all that matters.

It was a pity Blanche and Hannah were
taking extra practice sessions on the piano
during free time and weren't available to walk
with her. Mary always looked forward to

spending the free hour with her roommates, but it was a rare afternoon when both the music room and the instructor were available. She could have asked Charlotte at lunch, but now Mary did not know where she was. So Mary found herself on her own, with an unaccustomed longing to go outside but unable to do so without a companion.

Disappointed, Mary decided she might as well spend the time on her Braille. There was a sitting room off the hallway, where she and her roommates often went to sew or study. Mary used the guide rail as she walked in the direction of the room. When she reached a doorway, she put her hand on a small plaque by the doorjamb. Her Braille was by now at least good enough for her to read these room signs. Her fingers told her that this was the sitting room she had been looking for, and she stepped inside.

Mary liked this room because it had a comfortable window seat that she enjoyed curling up in. She paused to let a picture of the room come into her mind. Rooms in the college were arranged so that the furniture did not create unnecessary barriers that a student could walk into. This room had several armchairs arranged against the walls of the room. The window seat should be several feet away. From where she stood, Mary could not sense if there was anyone else already in the room.

"Hello?" she called. It used to embarrass Mary to call out to see if anyone was nearby. But everyone did that here at college, and Mary no longer felt strange finding herself saying hello to an empty room. However, this room turned out to not be empty, and Mary heard a boy's voice respond.

"Hello, Mary," the voice said.

Mary smiled at once.

"Hello, Ben," she said, proud at having recognized his voice.

"Ah, very good!" Ben exclaimed. "You can already tell us teaching assistants apart. And you've found your way here alone? You *are* settling in nicely. Soon you'll be one of the old hands here."

"Oh, I still need quite a bit of help," Mary

said warmly. "But yes, I did find this room on my own. I had been hoping for a walk, but my roommates are busy practicing their piano in the music room."

"You'd like to go outside?" Ben asked.

Mary's face flushed suddenly, and for a moment she thought Ben was going to offer to escort her. Surely that was against the rules! And even if it wasn't, Mary would never take a stroll with a boy she barely knew. Even if it was Ben Holden.

"There is a little seat by the garden door where students sit if they'd like to go walking but have no one to accompany them," Ben continued. "Usually another girl will come by hoping to find a walking partner, and out they go. There was someone there when I passed that way. If you'd like, I'll take you there, and we can see if she's still waiting. Then you'd have someone to walk with you."

"Thank you, that would be nice," Mary replied, relieved. Ben walked over and put his fingers lightly on the crook of Mary's arm, which made her face redden again.

"So how long have you been with us now?" Ben asked as they walked out of the sitting room.

"A little more than two weeks," Mary replied. "Although it seems much longer. I do feel more comfortable getting about, these days. I can go to a class alone if I have to, but usually one of my roommates is with me."

"You are very lucky to live with Blanche and Hannah," Ben said.

"Oh, I know it," Mary replied quickly. "I wasn't certain what to expect before coming here. And it has been difficult to be without my family. But Blanche and Hannah have made me feel at home. It has been hard sometimes, but never as bad as I thought it might be."

"You're lucky, then," Ben replied. "You may not realize it, Mary, but you are not exactly a run-of-the-mill new girl. Often students are quite terrified when they first arrive, and why shouldn't they be? To be blind, perhaps recently so, and to come live in an enormous building with so many strangers? I can think of several students who could not leave their rooms for the first week, from sheer terror. To have the confidence to walk to the sitting room alone, when you have been here only two weeks—well, you are unusual, Mary Ingalls. Not everyone finds things so easy."

Mary said nothing, but inside she felt confused. Mattie called her Miss Good Girl because she did not express bitterness about being blind—and now Ben thought things came easily to her, because she had already learned how to get around school alone. But neither one of these were actually true.

Things here do not come *that* easily, Mary thought angrily. I worked very hard to learn to walk these halls on my own. Why should it be that people think things are so easy for me on the inside, when they can only judge from what I show on the outside?

But Mary had no intention of letting Ben know that she was angry.

"It doesn't *all* come easily, I promise you," was all she said.

"Then you hide it well," Ben said with a laugh.

They walked in silence for a moment. Mary did not know what else to say.

"Ah, good, she is still sitting there," Ben said suddenly. "All bundled up for a walk. Will that wrap be enough for you, Mary? The rain has stopped, but it is still damp and chilly. It is December, after all."

"I'll be all right," Mary said. She wanted to go on only a short walk anyway.

"Look, Mattie, I have found you a walking companion."

Mary's heart sank. She had never thought to ask Ben who was waiting for a walk. Mattie was the *last* person in the world Mary wanted to walk with. But Ben had gone out of his way to bring her here, and she could hardly refuse to go now.

"Don't tell me that's Miss Good Girl Ingalls. Step into the light—why yes it is! I didn't ask you to bring her." Mattie's voice was its customary blend of cold, haughty, and irritated.

"You didn't ask me to do anything at all," Ben replied calmly. "I'm just trying to be helpful. You are sitting there wanting a walk, and have no one to go with you. Mary wants a walk and has no companion either. She's quite easy to get along with. Stop grumbling and have your walk."

Mary was surprised that Ben spoke in such a familiar way to Mattie. He seemed extremely polite when he spoke to Mary. Maybe he was accustomed to Mattie's rudeness, and simply responded in like fashion.

It was an awkward situation, and Mary felt an unexpected pang of sympathy for Mattie. Obviously Mattie was as unhappy about the situation as she was. Perhaps the easiest thing to do was to go ahead and take the walk.

"Well, I am here and you are here, and the truth is I should very much like a walk," Mary said.

"Wonderful," Ben exclaimed. "I'll leave you to your stroll, then."

He was gone before Mary could think of any reason to stop him.

"Always the nice one, aren't you, Mary Ingalls?" Mattie said. "Always unfailingly polite. As if you want to walk with me any more than I want to walk with you."

Now Mary wished she hadn't suggested they go. Why don't I ever say what I am really feeling? Mary wondered. If I did, I might not be stuck here with Mattie. I could have gone back to the sitting room and curled up in the window seat.

"Never mind, then," Mattie said suddenly, as if she sensed Mary's train of thought. "We might as well walk before the rain comes back. But don't expect me to chatter like one of your empty-headed roommates, and don't expect me to dither. I walk quickly, so if you can't keep up, don't come."

Mary was suddenly resolved to walk every bit as fast as Mattie, no matter how much effort it took.

"Let's go," Mary said, lifting her chin defiantly.

There was a blast of air as Mattie opened the door. It *was* cold out. More so than Mary liked. And the air felt damp and heavy, as if the clouds might burst open and rain down on them at any moment. But Mary wasn't going to change her mind now. Mattie would realize that Mary was no shrinking violet.

"It may rain soon," Mattie said as the door slammed shut behind them.

"I don't mind," Mary said.

"You'll mind when your dress needs pressing and your hair comes undone, Miss Good Girl," Mattie said.

"Don't call me that," Mary said. To her own ears, her voice sounded sharp and rude, but Mattie just laughed unkindly.

They walked in silence for a few minutes. Mattie had not taken Mary's arm, and Mary kept alongside by listening for the footsteps beside her. Unlike her roommates, or anyone else she had walked with while at college, Mattie said absolutely nothing about where they were going, or what their surroundings were like. She obviously did not intend to give Mary any help at all.

Very well, thought Mary. I will sort things out myself.

Miss Mattice had told Mary that there was a long, wide gravel walk in front of the main building, and that a popular walk followed a route around the grounds' cinder oval drive in the back. Mary guessed that was where they were going. Gravel crunched under her feet. The breeze smelled of wet earth and grass. The two girls walked for what seemed like a long time in total silence.

Mary felt a cold, fat raindrop land on the back of her neck. The wind picked up, hard enough for some of Mary's hair to come loose from its pins and blew into her face. Suddenly unnerved by the rapidly worsening weather, Mary lost her concentration and stumbled on the gravel. It began to sprinkle more steadily, and this made it hard to hear Mattie's foot-steps. Reaching out to the front and to the side with both arms, she felt nothing. A sudden wave of fear made her stomach churn.

"Mattie?" she called.

"I'm right here—you needn't scream at me," came Mattie's reply.

"I'm not screaming," Mary replied. She heard Mattie begin to walk again, and her panic began to return. Mary reached out and grabbed hold of the back of Mattie's wrap. Like it or not, Mattie was going to have to give Mary some assistance.

But Mattie set off walking much faster than Mary anticipated. She was left holding only the wrap in her hands, and in her surprise she dropped it.

"Give that back," Mattie cried.

"I didn't mean to take it in the first place," Mary retorted. "You walked away too quickly."

"Give it to me," Mattie said.

"I've dropped it," Mary said, leaning down to feel for the wrap. It had fallen onto the grass, which was still soaked from days of rain. She felt Mattie's hand roughly collide with her own as she snatched the wrap off the ground.

"It's wet now," Mattie said angrily. "And I told you before you would have to keep up with me. If you can't, you should have stayed inside with your beginning Braille reader, Miss Good Girl."

Mary's temper had been creeping out in little fits and starts for the last few minutes. Now it threatened to overtake her entirely. And she let it.

"Why do you call me that?" Mary cried. "It is unkind, and it isn't true. You don't even know me!"

"I know enough," Mattie shot back.

It was now raining heavily. The wind blew the raindrops in all directions.

"I know girls exactly like you, Mary Ingalls," Mattie continued. "All spine and rectitude, perfect manners, never a hair out of place. Cheerful and optimistic all the day long, come what may. When anyone with a lick of sense knows it is all an act!"

"What do you mean?" Mary asked, her voice shaking with anger and cold.

"You are blind, Mary Ingalls. *Blind!* And I am half blind, maybe more. Everything we were raised to know and expect has been ripped away from us. We have nothing, and we'll live to get nothing. We are charity cases!"

"I am *not* a charity case!" Mary exclaimed. "I am learning skills here that I can use in life so I will not be a burden to my family!"

"You will *always* be a burden to them, Mary! The rest is just nonsense the school spouts to keep us busy and to justify the money they charge to keep us here. Mr. Carothers and the rest of them can say what they like—the truth is we will never have normal lives. We will never become proper ladies, or have our own households, or children of our own. We will live with our families if they will have us, or in places like this if they won't. Because who else would want us now, Mary Ingalls? Even you, with your baby blue eyes and your blond hair. Even you, Mary Ingalls. What young man will have you now? None of them!"

Mattie was shouting now. Mary was stunned into silence by Mattie's tirade.

"Why do I call you Miss Good Girl?" Mattie continued. "Because you are one of those stupid girls who talk as if God did you a favor when he took away the life that you knew. Because you can't admit that something bad happened to you and that it isn't fair. Because you are a *liar*, Mary Ingalls."

"I'm not," Mary said, finding her voice. "I'm not any of those things."

"You *are*," Mattie shot back.

Mary was frozen. Her head was spinning. In her entire life, no one had ever spoken to her like this. She wanted to yell and slap and run away all at the same time.

"I'm *not!*" Mary shouted. "You're just angry and sour, Mattie. I can't help it if you've given up—I can't help it if your eyes look milky and strange!"

Mary wanted to bite back the words as soon as she'd said them. Angry as she was, she'd never meant to mention Mattie's eyes. It was cruel to have said what she had—there was no way around it.

"Find your own way home," Mattie said, her voice so low Mary almost didn't hear it.

Then she heard nothing but the raindrops pummeling the ground.

"I'm sorry. I shouldn't have said that," Mary said.

But there was no reply.

"Mattie?"

Surely she hadn't really meant for Mary to find her own way back. Even Mattie would not abandon Mary altogether. Would she?

Mary had a chilling realization that steadily grew. Mattie *had* left her here, in the freezing rain and the wind, uncertain in which direction the school lay.

"No," Mary said. "No! It isn't fair! It *isn't* fair!"

And she repeated those three words over and over again, shouting into the wind, tears mingling with raindrops on her face.

It isn't fair, none of it is—I'm not supposed to be here! I was going to be a teacher. I might have had a job by now. Perhaps be courted by a young man—I'm meant to have a family of my own!

How could anyone possibly know the enormity of Mary's loss? Even Laura, beloved Laura, could never fully understand how much Mary had lost when her eyes had failed, how much she had been forced to give up without question. The Ingallses had very little money. They all knew perfectly well that Mary would live with her parents or her sisters for the rest of her life, and she would be welcomed and loved there. But they did not know how it felt to have her own future stripped away—her independence. Nobody knew. Nobody understood how enraging it was. Nobody had ever fully acknowledged it.

Except Mattie.

Mary sobbed, bent over double with exhaustion and anger. She cried until she had nothing left inside her. Then she stood quietly in the rain, trying to catch her breath.

I must be calm, Mary told herself. I must think of the way that we came, and retrace those steps back to the garden door.

But in all the shouting and arguing, Mary had gotten turned around and confused. She did not know which way was forward and which was back. The main building could be anywhere. Mary wanted to scream. But an inner voice spoke soothingly to her.

You must find shelter. A place out of the wet and the cold. Calm down and use your ears to see. What do you hear?

I hear rain, Mary's voice screamed back inside her head. I hear wind.

Listen more carefully, said the calm inside voice. What is the rain hitting? What are you standing on? Where is the wind coming from?

Mary swallowed, shivering. She could tell she was standing on grass. She must have come slightly off the gravel path. The wind was no help—it blew from all directions at once. Mary listened keenly to the rain.

It was coming down hard all around her. For several moments, every beat sounded precisely like the one before. But then Mary noticed that when the wind picked up in a certain direction, she could hear a slightly different sound, as if the rain were hitting something solid. Mary listened intently, but she couldn't make anything out clearly.

Be patient, said the quiet inside voice. Use what you have. Don't be afraid to wait.

Mary wanted to swat the inside voice away. But at the moment it was her only source of advice, so she didn't.

There! The wind shifted and Mary heard the sound again. The rain was being blown against something that sounded like wood.

She was already lost, so Mary had no reason not to follow what she heard. Stretching her arms out in front, she made her way cautiously forward, fingertips extended. Step after step, Mary felt nothing.

She was about to turn and try a different

direction when a particularly strong burst of wind whipped the rain toward her. Mary knew the sound now, from every shanty her family had lived in. It was rain hitting a thin wooden roof. There was something there. Mary stepped forward, and her hands smacked into a wall.

Shaking with fatigue and excitement, Mary felt her way along the wall until her hands found a door. She fumbled with a latch, opened it, and half stepped, half fell inside. She pulled the door closed behind her and sank to the floor, numb with cold.

The last thing Mary remembered was the smell of clay pots and soil, and the thunderous drumming on the roof overhead. Then she heard nothing at all.

A voice was saying Mary's name from miles away.

I am dreaming, Mary thought. But what am I dreaming about?

"Mary, please try to answer me," the voice came again. "Mary Ingalls. Can you sit up at all? Are you hurt?"

Mary stirred and moved a little. She knew now who was saying her name—it was Ben Holden, his voice tight with worry.

"I . . . I'm just cold. I'll be fine," Mary said.

Mary felt a blanket being wrapped around her.

"Do you know where you are?" Ben asked.

Mary did not know where she was. But she did remember what had happened.

"We argued, Mattie and I. She ran off," Mary said.

"I know," Ben said.

How could Ben know?

"She was so angry, shouting and hollering at me. I lost my temper," Mary said. "I didn't mean to, I shouldn't have. But you don't know what she can be like, Ben."

"I do," Ben said wearily, helping Mary to her feet. "I know very well what she is like. Mattie is my sister."

A New Outlook

Mary had taken a chill, and Ben had walked her to the infirmary. She lay quite still in her bed, her unseeing eyes opened.

For all Mary knew, Mattie might be in the infirmary as well, even in the next bed. But she did not ask, or call out to see if anyone else was there. She said nothing at all, except for a murmured "Thank you" when the nurse came with a cup of hot tea.

Mary could not remember the last time she had shouted at someone in anger. Certainly she had not done so since she was a little girl. Had she ever done it? She was shaken by everything that had happened, by the hugeness of Mattie's anger and of her own, by the fear of being left alone in the freezing rainstorm, and by a sense of overwhelming sadness.

Mary had judged Mattie harshly for being an angry and unpleasant person. Now it seemed that Mary herself had been judged for hiding away her feelings about being blind. The worst part was that although she thought the secret of her feelings was buried safely inside her, she knew that some of what Mattie had said was true.

The scarlet fever had hit her so quickly. One minute she had been hanging clothes out to dry, and the next she was in bed with a head that ached so badly, it seemed unbearable. Everything that followed was a blur. Mary remembered very little of it.

When the fever had begun to fade, Mary had known something was not right. Her eyes did not work as they used to. Mary felt as if she was looking at everything through a pane of sooty glass. And each day, the world had faded a little more from her sight.

By the second day after the fever broke, Mary knew she was going blind. She had seen many families over the years that had been struck by scarlet fever. Many people, especially children, died from it. And ones who lived sometimes went blind. Mary knew that this was what was happening to her, and she guessed Ma and Pa knew as well, though they did not discuss it. Mary drank in everything she could with her eyes during those days. She looked at things fiercely, as if she could burn the faces of her family into her mind forever. The last thing Mary could remember seeing was the deep lake blue of her sister Grace's eyes.

In the days that followed, Mary was still too weak to get out of bed. She floated in and out of sleep, and once she heard Ma crying quietly. She knew that Ma was crying because Mary would never see again. And Mary heard Pa say softly, "But she is alive, Caroline. We have not lost her. Remember that. God has spared Mary's life, and we must be thankful for it."

Ma and Pa had lost one child already. Mary had only been ten when her baby brother,

Freddie, had died, but Ma's and Pa's quiet grief, dark and deep as a well, was something Mary could never forget. From that day on, remembering Pa's words to Ma, Mary thought of her blindness as the price she had paid to live. Ma and Pa, who always taught their children never to dwell on sadness, put the best face on things themselves and acted cheerful. Mary knew they expected the same from her. "God never closes a door without somewhere opening a window," Ma would say. And Mary knew that the door God had closed was her sight, and the opened window was her life.

But deep inside, Mary *was* angry. And she felt great guilt when this anger flared up. It did not seem right to feel angry when her life had been spared, and she was surrounded and supported by a loving family. So she quashed the angry feelings away, and she never told anyone about them. Only Mary herself knew what she truly felt.

She remembered the inner flames that had eaten away at her in the dark days following her recovery from the scarlet fever, the dark, bubbling pools of rage. Moments when she wanted to slap Ma's gently attending hands away. When she felt hatred for eyes that now served no purpose but to produce tears that she had to rub away and hide. Eyes that everyone had always told her were so lovely.

Gradually, Mary won the battle against her rage. She grew to take pride in the fact that she did not complain about what had happened, and outwardly faced the world with optimism and cheer. She had gone on acting like the good and obedient girl that she had always been before she got sick.

And really, what else could she have done, at home among her family? They could not bring Mary's sight back. Sharing how lost, how miserable and damaged she felt, would only have grieved them. That was not something Mary wanted to bring to her family.

But she wasn't with her family now. She was with a different group of people, girls and boys who all, in one way or another, shared something with Mary. They weren't brought together by a last name or a homestead, but by blindness. Mary had come to college to learn Braille, to find ways to function and care for herself now that she was blind, and to get the education she longed for. But perhaps there was something else to be had here that Mary had never considered. This was an opportunity for Mary to be understood in a way she never could be back at home. And just maybe, this was also a place where those long-ago, locked-away emotions might safely be let out.

Though Mary felt much better after her rest and her hot tea, the nurse insisted she remain overnight in the infirmary, in case she developed a temperature. Mary slept fitfully, dreaming that Mattie had chased her out into the prairie, then left her alone as a prairie fire raged toward her. Mary had lived through prairie fires before, and the one in her dream seemed as scorching and terrifying as the real thing. But in the dream, even as the flames grew closer and closer, Mary held her ground. She stood and fought the fire with blankets, and buckets of water, and finally her own two feet—stamping the flames out. And at some point during the dream, Mary realized that she could see. The flames, her fighting with them, had somehow opened her eyes and restored her sight.

But it was only a dream. When Mary awakened in the morning, nothing had changed. Physically, she felt well enough. She knew she was not going to take sick. No student could leave the infirmary without the okay of the nurse, who was supposed to be checking on Mary shortly. Dressed and ready to go, Mary was sitting on her bed patiently, her mind buzzing with thoughts, when she heard footsteps crossing the wooden floor. Not the nurse, Mary thought. Someone younger and quicker.

"Is Mary Ingalls well enough for a visitor?"

It was Ben Holden. Mary was surprised and taken aback. She had not thought she would be facing Mattie's brother so soon.

"Hello, Ben. I was expecting the nurse. I'm supposed to go back to class as soon as she gives me permission."

"I'm glad to see you looking so well," Ben said.

Mary knew he only meant that she had not taken ill, but her cheeks prickled with heat at the compliment.

"I was concerned that you would have a fever or cough after getting so wet and cold last night. It was dreadful of Mattie to leave you alone. You must have been frightened out of your wits! Mattie came to me straight away when she got inside, to tell me what she had done and ask me to go outside to find you. She had gone back herself calling for you, but you were already gone. I don't believe Mattie meant you any real harm. But that doesn't change what she did. I have to say I feel partly responsible for what happened, sending you on the walk with her. I know my sister can be very ill-tempered, but I never imagined she would do something so reckless."

"I'm also partly to blame," Mary said quickly. "I said something cruel to her, about her eyes. And since she knows I can't see her face, it was obvious that someone else had told me that her eyes didn't look right, that people had been talking about her. I was told how sensitive she is about her appearance, and I said something about it anyway. Whatever else happened, I do want to apologize to her for that."

"I'm afraid you won't have the chance," Ben said.

"Why not?" Mary asked, confused. "Has something happened to her?"

"Mattie has been asked to leave," Ben said. "She will not be continuing as a student here."

"But why? Is it because of last night—is it because of me?"

"Mattie and Mr. Carothers and Miss Mattice had a long talk last night, after I found you and brought you to the infirmary. This isn't the first time Mattie's behavior has come to their attention. She's been given several warnings in the past. It's been agreed now that it is not in anyone's best interest, including Mattie's, for her to stay here."

At first, Mary felt only overwhelming relief that Mattie was gone. Mary would never have to come face-to-face with her again, would no longer have to bear her taunts. But the relief was tinged with guilt. She had made Mattie angrier, after all, and maybe pushed her over the edge. Mary had never imagined that Mattie would have to leave college. It was a disgrace to be sent away, and as much as she hated Mattie, Mary had never wanted something like this to happen.

"Where will she go?" Mary asked.

"Home, for now," Ben replied. "Our family lives close by. I don't know what will happen next. There is another school for the blind in Boston. Perhaps Mattie will go there. Or it may be that Mattie is better off away from other blind people. They may be too painful a reminder of her own affliction. But don't worry, Mary. Our family is comfortably off. Mattie will always be taken care of."

That is exactly what she doesn't want, Mary thought.

"Can I speak to her before she goes?" Mary asked.

"I've just come from seeing her off," Ben said. "The college driver is taking her home."

"I don't understand how this has all been decided so fast."

"Not as fast as you may think, Mary. Since coming to college, Mattie has driven three different roommates away, and lashed out at others at meals and in the classroom. It was made very clear to Mattie that if she misbehaved again, she would have to leave. She was very nearly sent away several months ago, but the college agreed to keep her on as long as I was here to temper her behavior. We all hoped that being here would be helpful to Mattie, that she would meet others and be able to share her experiences with them. Mattie was not like this before her . . . illness. But ever since, she has been terribly angry and wanted no help or comfort from anyone. Before the disease struck her eyes, Mattie was engaged to be married. She expected a lavish wedding and an easy life full of beautiful things in a luxurious home. She wanted to have many children. But when her sight began to fail, the young man ended the engagement."

"But that isn't right!" Mary said. "If this man wanted to marry Mattie, the illness shouldn't have made a difference."

"I happen to agree with you, Mary. It was a very cruel thing. But it did make a difference to him, and what's done is done."

"I didn't know about her broken engagement," Mary said. "It might have helped me to understand her better."

"Mattie doesn't want to be understood, Mary, and she doesn't want to be helped. And until that changes, no one's good intentions can help her."

Mary knew that was true, but nonetheless she felt ashamed. She had not meant well toward Mattie until this moment. She had hated her. She had been relieved to hear of her departure. It had never occurred to Mary to wonder if there was something behind Mattie's miserable behavior.

Is a tragic tale what entitles someone to my friendship? Mary thought. Shouldn't I have given Mattie the benefit of the doubt *without* knowing her story?

"Well, I just wanted to make sure that you suffered no serious illness from last night," Ben said. "I have a great deal to take care of today. I will also be going home as soon as Mr. Carothers finds a replacement for me."

"Are you leaving the college as well, Ben?" Mary asked.

"I am," Ben replied. "I have worked here only to be close to Mattie, though she did not want me. She could not stop me from getting a job here, but she forbade me to tell anyone she was my sister, and usually rejected any help I tried to give her. But I had to try. And I will keep trying."

"You're a very good person," Mary said.

"Oh, I don't know about that," Ben replied. "But I am a lucky one. Good-bye, Mary."

"Good-bye," she replied quietly.

After Ben left, Mary sat lost in thought. She had come to the Iowa College for the Blind with the firm resolve to do things well and without mistakes. How foolish she had been. Not for making mistakes, or failing to be fault-less, but because she had thought perfection so important in the first place.

The only mistake Mary now truly regretted was closing her heart to another person. And not just any person, but a girl her own age who had suffered a loss very similar to her own. Why had she not known better? Why had she not remembered her own feelings and recognized the same ones in Mattie?

All the compassion Mary had denied Mattie now bubbled to the surface, and she cried for the miserable girl who had left college in disgrace.

If only I could tell her, Mary thought. If only I could just talk to her. But Mattie is gone, and it is too late.

But Mary was still here. All the opportunity Mattie had squandered was still Mary's to seize.

For Mary, it was not too late to make a fresh start.

At Home

After several days had passed, Mary told Blanche and Hannah what had really happened the night she was caught in the rain. Hannah had been outraged, but Mary kept shushing her until she had told the entire story, including how she had been able to figure out where she was and find shelter on her own, a point she was particularly proud of, and how Mattie had gone back to find her.

"You were remarkably brave and clever, Mary. Thank goodness you found that shed! Still, you trusted Mattie, and she abandoned you in the pouring rain. Why do you sound so forgiving? I'm glad she's gone!" Hannah declared emphatically.

"Oh, Hannah, please don't say that."

"But that's how I feel," Hannah insisted. "And don't tell me you don't feel the same, Mary Ingalls. Don't tell me you aren't happy Mattie is gone for good."

Mary sighed.

"It's true, Hannah. I do feel relieved that Mattie has left. But I've come to realize that Mattie wasn't as bad as I thought she was. She tried to make it right soon afterward, coming back out to look for me. And when she couldn't find me, she went to her brother. Ben told me Mattie knew she was on very thin ice with the college, and that one more incident would be enough to have her expelled. Mattie would have known that when she told Ben what she'd done. But she did it anyway, to make sure someone would rescue me."

"I think you're being more than fair to Mattie," Blanche said. "But if you believe there is some good in her, then I do as well."

"I don't," Hannah exclaimed. "I tell you, we

are better off without her."

"That is probably true, Hannah, but it shouldn't stop us from having some understanding, even some forgiveness for Mattie. She is gone now, but there are other Matties in the world, and we may well meet some of them right here. And I, for one, intend to do things differently next time."

"But what is there to understand?" Hannah asked. "Mattie was just horrible, plain and simple. We didn't cause her to act that way. When she first arrived, everyone tried to be kind to Mattie. But after a time, we realized there was no point. She went right on being nasty for no reason."

"But there's more to the story that we didn't know," Mary said gently. "And since Mattie isn't coming back, I don't think it would be wrong to tell you now."

Mary and her roommates were curled by the fire in one of the smaller reading rooms. At the moment, they were the only students there, so Mary spoke freely about Mattie's plans to be married, and how her fiancé had left her.

"Oh dear," Hannah said. "That *is* a very sad thing. What a cold man he must have been."

"Think of it. As Mattie is still getting used to the fact that her sight is permanently damaged and she may one day be fully blind, she then has her entire future snatched away from her. Can you imagine what that did to Mattie's spirit?"

"Filled it with rage," Blanche said quietly. "Is that what you mean, Mary? That Mattie became the horrible girl we knew *because* of all this."

"I can't pretend to know that Mattie was an entirely warm and loving person before this happened," Mary said. "But yes, I do believe that losing her eyesight and her fiancé embittered her deeply."

Hannah made an unhappy noise in her throat.

"Well I feel perfectly *wretched* now," she whimpered.

Mary sidled closer to Hannah and put her arm around her.

"Don't feel wretched, Hannah. That wasn't why I told you the story. I just felt it was important to make you understand about

Mattie. I know it has made a great difference to me. And I will remember that what a person seems on the surface always holds a story, and that not all those stories are pleasant."

"We'll all remember that, Mary," Blanche said. "Thank you for telling us her story. I shall remember Mattie in my prayers. Perhaps she will be happy again one day."

The fire crackled quietly, punctuated periodically by one of Hannah's sniffs.

"I went blind all at once, after I fell from an apple tree and hit my head on a wheelbarrow," Hannah said after a few moments. "I was younger than you were when you took the scarlet fever, Mary. I was just seven. I remember at first simply not understanding why it had been night for so long, why no one would light a lantern. I kept asking my ma why it wasn't morning yet, and why the horses were trotting by on the lane outside in the middle of the night. It wasn't until I heard my brothers and sisters leaving for school that I began to realize something wasn't right. That the world was working properly, but my eyes weren't.

And still, no one told me what was happening. I thought my eyes had bruises on them, and I kept asking Ma when they would be better again. Nobody ever told me I was blind. Even when they talked among themselves, my parents never used that word."

Mary had never heard good-natured Hannah sound angry before.

"Maybe they didn't know, Hannah," Blanche said. "They might have been hoping it was only temporary, and didn't want to frighten you."

"Well, they did frighten me by saying nothing—I thought the sun had gone out!" Hannah retorted. "One day my five-year-old sister asked if I would remember what she looked like, how did she put it—'now that your eyes are broken, Hannah.' That was the day I realized I wasn't ever going to see again. I had to figure that out *myself*—a seven-year-old girl."

"That was wrong of your ma," Mary said. "I'm sure she was trying her best to keep you from pain, but she did the wrong thing."

"My story is nowhere near as dramatic,"

Blanche said. "There is a great deal of vision loss in my family. I have two blind aunts, a blind granny, and several cousins who are only partially sighted. I grew up being comfortable around blind people, and also knowing that it was possible one day I would lose my sight. I wasn't like Mattie at all. I never dared to plan for a future that I knew might not come. When the doctor told me that I was in the first stages of blindness, I cried. Do you know why?"

"You were afraid and angry, of course," Mary said.

"I was a little afraid," Blanche said. "But that wasn't why I cried. It seems so silly now, but we had the sweetest dog, a bloodhound named Bo. He was—he is still—the smartest and most loyal dog I've ever known. When I was a girl, I felt Bo could understand my thoughts and feelings in a way no one else could. We would go for walks and sit by a stream, and I would look into Bo's huge, brown eyes, and he would look back at me. Strange as it sounds, it felt as if we were talking to each other. Bo was the first thing I thought of when the doctor told me. I was crying at the possibility that I would not be able to look into those eyes anymore."

From beside the fireplace came a small sob.

"Oh, Hannah, you silly goose. You needn't cry about it. Bo is still alive and well, though a little older and stiffer, and when I'm home, we still go on those walks. And now, instead of looking into those brown eyes, I let Bo use them to guide me. He always takes me straight to our spot by the stream, and I know I am absolutely safe with him."

"He sounds wonderful, Blanche," Mary said, thinking wistfully of Jack.

"He is, Mary. I hope you will meet him someday."

Hannah gave a deep, emotional sigh.

"When I was first strong enough to be out of bed after the scarlet fever," Mary said, "Ma would take my sisters out of the house so that I could practice finding my way around by touch. You'd think when you live in such a small place, and you knew where everything was when you could see, that it would be easy to find your way around blind. But it wasn't. I'd think a wall was seven steps away, and it would turn out to be only four. Which means, of course, that I'd walk into it. I would have my hands out to touch the mantelpiece, when I was actually nowhere near. It was so frustrating."

"It has been hard," Blanche said softly, placing her hand on Mary's arm.

"It has," Mary agreed. "But tonight, look at me! A college girl, sitting snug by the fire with two good friends! What more could I want?"

Hannah laughed, and reached to hug Mary. Mary felt contentment spread over her. It was almost Christmas week, and today the first snowfall had come. Blanche and Hannah were coming to feel more like sisters to her each day. Things had been difficult, and might be again. But tonight, all was well.

Mary sat on the edge of her bed. She was suddenly taken back to her first day at the Iowa College for the Blind, when she had sat in this very spot waiting for someone to come and find her. Now the room seemed oddly empty with Blanche and Hannah gone. Mary had plenty to do in Vinton over the Christmas holiday. She had volunteered to help two of the younger students who were also spending their first holidays away from home. Mary had proved to have an excellent command of geography in her political economy class, and Miss Mattice had asked her to tutor the two girls. Mary loved the map molds that were used at the college. They used different textures and raised areas to convey mountains and flatlands, oceans, and continents by touch. Braille text labeled countries and states. The college even had a large tactile globe made of wood, which students could run their hands over to feel and understand the layout of their world. Mary knew she would enjoy sharing her knowledge of geography with the younger girls, and helping them to learn the countries and states by touch. She would not only be tutoring the girls, but be acting as a big sister to them during their first holiday alone. Mary knew she would do this well.

Mary was also looking forward to the

departure from the daily academic schedule. There would be a special Christmas dinner, followed by a fiddle concert. Several of the reading rooms would have fires in the hearth at all hours of the day, and Miss Mattice had said that students would be permitted to pop corn if they liked. So there would be good company and food, and plenty to do.

Still, Mary could not help but feel a little gloomy. She had eagerly followed her family's Christmas preparations through the letters that came regularly from home. Ma had written her about a secret she was keeping—she had bought a beautiful book of poetry for Laura and hidden it away in a drawer. Ma confessed she was having a dreadful time not telling Laura about it, because she knew how thrilled she was going to be. By now Ma and Laura would have finished making the red and white striped Christmas paper that all the Ingalls gifts were wrapped in every year. Carrie would be showing Grace the way to make molasses-on-snow candy, and how to press thimbles into frosted snowpanes to form lovely patterns in the windows. And the Ingallses would be popping corn too, to make popcorn balls with molasses and brown sugar.

All without Mary.

Well, it *is* a shame, Mary thought. I would rather be home than at school, and I won't pretend otherwise. It is strange being at college with the buildings half empty of students, and it is lonely thinking of my family having their celebration so far away from me. But I will have my two young students to help, and with our studying I will take their minds off their families as best I can. At the very least, I can tell them I understand how they are feeling, and mean it.

The stay-overs were scheduled to meet in the main study hall, and that was where Mary was supposed to meet her young charges.

I'll just sit here a few more minutes before going down, Mary thought, imagining I am at home right now. Ma is singing by the stove, and everything smells of cranberries and cake and roasting meat.

Mary's inner world of cheerful sounds and

smells was interrupted by a knock on the door.

"Come in," she said, reaching up quickly to smooth her hair.

"Why, Mary, you look a thousand miles away!"

Mary laughed. "I guess in a way I was, Miss Mattice," she said. "I was thinking of what my family is doing at this very moment, on Christmas Eve."

"Well, it's not a wonder you had such a big smile on your face," Miss Mattice replied warmly. Mary felt a pressure on the bed as her teacher came and sat down beside her.

"I wanted to thank you for volunteering to help Tessie and Lucia," Miss Mattice said. "Poor girls, they are so young, and they have never been separated from their families before. It will be very hard for them tonight and tomorrow on Christmas Day, as I expect you well know yourself."

"Oh, I do. I *have* been feeling sad," Mary said. "No matter what we do here, it won't be the same as being home. Not for any of us. But I am glad to be able to help, honestly."

"I've brought you some mail, Mary," Miss Mattice said. "And a package from home!"

Mary's heart skipped a beat. She had been hoping that her family would send her a Christmas present, but now that Christmas Eve had come, she had given up hoping that a package might arrive. And here it was!

"There are two letters in addition to the package. One is from Laura, and one is from your Ma. Would you like to hear them?"

Naturally, Mary wanted to hear them as soon as possible, and she also wanted to rip open her package to find out what was inside. But that would leave her nothing to savor on Christmas Day. If she waited, she would be able to luxuriate all night in the knowledge that on Christmas she would have both letters *and* a gift from home! It would be well worth the wait, Mary decided. Besides, Tessie and Lucia would be down in the main study hall soon, waiting for her.

"Thank you, Miss Mattice, but I think I'll save them for tomorrow. It will feel a little more like a proper Christmas that way."

"I admire your willpower, Mary," Miss Mattice said cheerfully. "Would you like to go down to meet your young charges together?"

"I'll sit and enjoy the quiet just a few minutes longer, if that's all right," Mary said.

Miss Mattice stood up, then leaned down to hug Mary. She placed Mary's package and letters on her lap.

"I know you expected a great deal from yourself when you arrived here as a new student," Miss Mattice said. "And I have come to expect quite a lot from you as well. You never disappoint me. We are quite lucky to have you here at the Iowa College for the Blind, Mary. I think this will be a better place for your presence."

Mary glowed with pleasure. She returned Miss Mattice's hug enthusiastically.

"I know it isn't your Ma and Pa's house, Mary, but we do have a few treats in store for you and all the stay-overs in the next few days. Come downstairs when you can."

"Thank you, Miss. Thank you for everything, truly."

Mary could feel the smile in Miss Mattice's voice.

"Merry Christmas, Mary."

Miss Mattice pulled the door closed with a squeak, and Mary listened for a moment to the fading footsteps. She ran her hands over the package and held one of the envelopes close to her nose. Mary was sure she could detect the faint scent of home on the paper. Again, she touched the paper-wrapped package, knowing Ma's hands had touched it too. Mary could finally enjoy her college Christmas now, knowing she had some family Christmas waiting in her room.

Mary placed the letters on her bed alongside the package. She straightened her skirts and left her room. She really didn't need the guide rail now. She knew every step, every turn, every drafty spot between here and the study hall. But she let her fingers brush the top of the guide rail anyway, enjoying the highly polished smoothness so many fingers had left on the wood.

As she approached the study hall, she could hear that there were already quite a few people inside. Mary entered the room, pausing just inside the doorway to give her senses a moment to take in the information. There were voices singing a carol loudly and a little off-key. She could smell the smoke from the hearth, along with the scent of popping corn. There was laughing, warmth, and a buzz of activity. The sounds and smells were both strange and familiar. They were echoes of the sensations she knew from past holidays at home. The room was different, the voices were different, even the scent of freshly baked gingerbread was not quite like Ma's.

And yet, really, it did feel like home.